SEA OF CHANGE

SHELLEY MUNRO

MUNRO PRESS

DEDICATION

For Paul, my husband, partner in crime, and fellow
adventurer.
Every day is a good day.

INTRODUCTION

A sexy face in the crowd...

Shifter Asia Bolino can't believe the gorgeous cutie is
Roman Anderson. They belong to enemy tribes, but she'd
love to run her fingers over his...assets. Roman doesn't
recognize her, and in a moment of weakness, Asia agrees
to a late-night date, a little forbidden pleasure.

Someone attacks Roman while he waits for Asia. Aware of his shifter status, Asia does the only thing she can—she takes him back to her apartment. The problem is that he thinks they're married when he regains consciousness. He parades around her apartment wearing nothing but a smile, and Asia is weak. She succumbs to his charm and skillful loving. Hip-deep in lies, she's aware the sensual bubble might burst at any moment. That might mean bloodshed, and she can't allow that to happen. Worse, Roman doesn't recall he's a shifter.

Asia struggles with guilt while melting at Roman's touch. Nothing can come of their relationship, and now it seems someone knows the truth, and they're both in danger.

Note to Readers

Shapeshifters fascinate me. This love of shifters started during my teenage years when I grabbed any available romance with shifter characters. I enjoyed the alpha male characters, how they valued family, and when they spotted their mate...wow! The intensity of the relationships, the thrills, the danger, and the adventure. I was hooked, so it made sense I'd gravitate to paranormal romance and shapeshifters when I began writing books. I've written werewolves, feline shapeshifters, dragons, and this one, which you'll see is a little different...

Remember join my newsletter
(https://shelleymunro.com/newsletter/)
to receive book news, details of promotions, and
information about new releases.

CHAPTER ONE

*W*ell, hello, gorgeous.

Asia Bolino tried not to stare as she slid into the Norah Jones number, following the cue from the accompanying musician. Her heart shifted into an erratic gallop while a wave of heat engulfed her body. *Turn around*, she pleaded silently. *Oh, looking good. Go on. Turn right around. Let me get a good look at you...*

Aw, rats!

Disappointment throbbed through her voice before she pulled herself together and continued singing the song in her husky voice. She knew that face, and the man was off limits. Way off limits.

Roman Anderson.

What was he doing slumming in the Blue Venetian nightclub?

Her mother would have a conniption if she became involved with an Anderson. Ah well. No harm in appreciating the view. Because there was no getting away from it—the man was a fine specimen. To hear her family talk, he was the devil incarnate, but jeepers, the man oozed sex appeal. She sucked in a breath as she viewed his rear end. Yep, looking good from all angles.

Asia held the final note before letting it trail away. The music ended, and she smiled at the audience, graciously accepting the applause with a regal incline of her head.

Roman Anderson was not the man for her. She sighed, accepting but not liking the truth. Feuds were the pits, especially when they limited the gene pool for shapeshifters like her. The warring between the Transient Orcas and the Resident Orcas was stupid and meaningless in these modern times, but Asia knew some actively encouraged the rift between the tribes.

The introductory bars of another Norah Jones favorite

pulled Asia back to professionalism. She started to sing in her trademark smoky voice, pleading the audience to come away with her. The low buzz of chatter in the nightclub faded, letting Asia know she was doing well. She let her eyes drift closed, threw back her head, and poured her heart out in the music.

For the three minutes of the song, she held the audience enthralled. The music faded, and for a heartbeat, there was total silence before the applause broke out. Asia's eyes popped open. She grinned and bowed from the waist, giving the group of businessmen at the front table, Roman Anderson included, an excellent view of her creamy cleavage. She straightened, snagging Roman's gaze for a long, drawn-out moment. He closed one brown eye in a wink and smiled at her—a drop-your-panties kind of smile—robbing her of breath.

Maybe he was adopted. *She could corrupt him*, she thought, taking half a step toward him before commonsense kicked her in the gut.

"That's the end of Scarlet's segment for now," an announcer said over the loudspeaker. "She'll be back for another at midnight."

Asia stepped down from the stage and headed to the bar for her customary glass of sparkling water. She leaned against the shiny, wooden bar and inhaled, wanting to fan the heat from her cheeks. She resisted, a little pique pulling at her customary poise. A man hadn't affected her this way since her ill-fated romance with her ex-manager. She should know better than to lust after a pretty face.

Asia waited while Frank, the barman, served a group of young women out for a bachelorette's party, judging by the screeching and laughter. She noticed several women eyeing Roman, offering flirtatious smiles and flicking luxurious locks. Nope, none of her business. But she couldn't prevent the satisfaction that stole through her when Roman ignored their overtures.

"Hey, Frank. It's busy tonight," she said when he finished serving the rush of customers. The sharp tang of whiskey contrasted with the sweetness of the floral scent wafting from the young women standing beside her.

"Sure is, Scarlet." Frank placed a glass in front of her. "Looks like someone is trying to grab your attention." He gestured behind her with a jerk of his blond head.

Asia smelled the green, fresh scent of the outdoors, seconds before the warm muskiness of a male body hit her with a whoosh. Trapped between the man's heat and the bar, she turned, ready to protest.

"Sorry, Scarlet." Roman's voice was husky and strummed pleasantly across her nerves. It matched the sexy body perfectly. "I didn't mean to crowd you. Someone pushed me." His brown eyes twinkled down at her, a novel experience for Asia since she hit six feet in her bare feet and towered over most men.

"Not that I'm sorry. You feel as good as you look."

An uncustomary blush climbed her neck and seeped into her cheeks, and she barely suppressed her sigh. Why did the enemy have to look so sexy? So tempting?

"No problem," she drawled, pausing to sip icy water. The cool liquid soothed her fluster until she glanced at Roman again. Shoot. He wanted her as much as she wanted him. And he had no idea of her identity. So what did she do now?

Play safe and tell him she wasn't interested, or walk on the wild side?

"My name is Roman Anderson." He held out his hand to cement the formal introductions.

"Scarlet," Asia said with a note of caution.

"Pleased to meet you, Scarlet. Could I interest you in a late supper after you finish here?"

His eyes narrowed as his attention zoomed in on her other hand. He picked it up and caressed the knuckles, his thumb strumming across the ruby and diamond band her grandmother had given her, and she always wore on her left hand. The ring helped scare away non-desirables, and if they were too thick to notice, she pointed it out to them.

"Or am I too late and someone has snapped you up already?"

This time, she went with honesty. "I'm not married."

"No man in your life?" His alert expression told her he was weighing her reply, judging if she told the truth.

She shook her head, letting the truth shine through. "I don't get much time to date." In this, at least, she could state the facts.

"Do you have time tonight?"

A negative reply formed in her mind. "Yes," she whispered.

Oh boy. Ma would lock her up and throw away the key. Except...

Asia thought rapidly and decided that one night with Roman Anderson was worth the risk. The family was away, and she didn't expect them back until the following month. And if they did arrive back unexpectedly, they rang first. Nine out of ten times, anyway, because they knew she had a hectic schedule. Her mother had muttered something about having a yearning for the fish off the coast of South America. They'd no doubt sample the local delicacy of seal meat while basking in the foreign waters.

One date.

Asia glanced at Roman's dark, handsome face. Hard to believe he was the killer whale monster depicted by her family. Where was the harm in one date? And maybe a little action between the sheets if they were of the same accord?

"Yes," she repeated in a firm voice.

"Great." Roman didn't act like her acceptance was a given, and she liked that. "Where should I meet you?"

Asia hesitated, trying to figure out how to maintain secrecy yet not tip Roman off that things weren't quite legitimate. "How about outside the side entrance at one?"

"I'll be there," he promised, his dark eyes glowing. "I'm looking forward to getting to know you. Very much."

A frisson of pure lust swept Asia. Her gaze drifted across his face, his mouth, and she wondered what it would feel like to touch him, to lean her weight into his chest and feel the dense muscles crush her breasts.

The soft clearing of a throat jerked her back to the present. Amusement coated his smile, bringing a renewed flush of heat to her face.

"Hold that thought." He blew her a kiss before returning to his table.

Asia groaned, her heart thumping so hard it felt as if she'd just finished a hundred-meter sprint. The last segment of her act couldn't finish soon enough.

Roman let his gaze wander over Scarlet. Statuesque. Curvy. Striking red hair that matched her name. He wondered if the color was real before deciding it didn't matter. The woman oozed confidence along with sexual allure, enthralling the audience with her husky voice. It thrummed through him, jerking his cock tight in pleasurable anticipation. He hadn't come into the nightclub to find a woman, but one look at Scarlet had changed his mind.

"Nice-looking lady," the man to his right murmured after noting the direction of Roman's gaze.

Damn, he didn't like being so transparent. Not when there was business involved.

"Yeah," he said, aware he couldn't push away the man without a comment. The need to dispose of the treasure was too critical. Thankfully, the two weeks of delicate negotiations were almost over, and he could return home soon. "I spoke to her when I went up to the bar. Intelligent woman."

"Pity," the man said with a laugh. "Sometimes, uncomplicated sex is best."

"I'll admit I was tempted," Roman said with a shrug. Instinct made him skirt the truth, the fact that he was meeting her later and hoped to round off the evening with a hot and heavy session in the sack. "But once I wrap up our business discussions, I'm heading back to the island. Duty calls. I'll have to forego pleasure this time around."

"Yeah, I heard you live on Auckland Island. Secluded place. What's it like?"

"Some people call it the end of the Earth. My family has lived there for generations. We like it. It's home."

And perfect for their shapeshifting species—the Resident Orcas. Most of them owned land in New Zealand, some in Australia, and farther afield, but they all returned to the secluded Auckland Islands, deep in the Southern Ocean, where they could change at will, frolic and hunt in the ocean without fear of detection.

"Modern technology must have brought you closer," the man observed.

"Sure. With helicopters and small planes, we're not so cut off from the mainland." But the island still ran on a feudal system, and as head of the tribe, he was fighting off a small, vocal group who didn't like the old ways.

Roman fought a scowl at the thought. Unfortunately, he was the only one who could negotiate the sale of the treasure, and his trip to the mainland was one he couldn't avoid. According to his brother, things were still under control on the island, albeit a bit tense between shifters with opposing viewpoints. Increasing numbers of shark mercenaries were also visiting the island, something

Roman didn't like. He was going to have to take action against the outspoken leaders before they ripped the tribe apart. The split that had occurred thousands of years ago in their species had done enough harm. He wouldn't put the tribe through the same turmoil again.

"Hell, I envy the man who goes to bed with her each night," the man said in a change of subject.

Roman nodded, his gaze on Scarlet while she performed an old Marilyn Monroe number. His breath caught halfway up his throat while his body reacted again in a purely sexual manner. Damn. A woman hadn't affected him in this way since his early teens. Roman couldn't wait to see where their date would lead.

Asia stepped out of her dressing room and headed through the bar. Now empty except for the cleaners, and with the lights on full, the room seemed sad and tacky, like a woman dressed way too young for her age. A vacuum cleaner hummed, and the clinking of glasses sounded as Frank stacked them into the glass washing machine.

"Night," she called to Frank.

"See you next week," he answered before continuing with his cleaning behind the bar.

Asia waved and headed for the side door that opened into a small alley.

Anticipation thrummed through her. Nervous, she licked her lips and wiped moist palms across the seat of her black trousers. She'd left on the red wig, conscious that Roman might recognize the long black hair or at least consider her and shapeshifters for a fleeting moment. She didn't want the date to end before it began. Like many female Orcas, Asia had a lock of white hair at her temple. It looked both distinctive and striking against her black hair. Since she worked on the mainland, Asia dyed it black to avoid speculation. She thanked the impulse that had led her to touch up her roots this morning because Roman would recognize the significance of the lock of white hair.

Asia slipped out the side door and paused to allow her eyes to adjust to the dimmer light. At the far end of the small alley, illumination from a streetlamp spilled in from the main street. Asia heard the rumble of a car before it turned into the adjacent street and faded, leaving a throbbing silence.

Fumes from rotten food rose from the large rubbish bin between her and the alley's exit. A shadow shifted, separating from the brick wall of the nightclub.

Roman was waiting for her.

A combination of relief and excitement fizzled through

her veins. Asia paused to take a deep breath, knowing she was running a risk yet unable to withstand the temptation. A woman would need to be stark raving mad to turn down a date with the sexy Roman.

A metallic clang broke the night. A shout. The smack of fist against flesh. Asia rounded the bin at a sprint and saw three dark-clad men attacking Roman.

"Hey!" she hollered. "Stop that!"

Two of the men paused while the third slammed a fist into Roman's belly and kicked him viciously. Roman fell, his head colliding with the footpath with a sickening thump.

Asia rushed forward, screeching at the top of her voice. "Fire! Fire! Someone help. There's a fire!"

One of the men spoke in a low, guttural voice—too low for Asia to catch the words. She kept running and almost turned her ankle in a pothole. *Damn high heels.*

"Fire!" she shouted, righting herself and ignoring the pain in her panic to stop them from hurting Roman.

The three men melted into the darkness, but not before one of them kicked Roman several times in the ribs. Asia leaped at him, ready to do some damage of her own, but he was too strong and thrust her away like an unwanted piece of litter. Her butt hit the footpath with enough force to jar her entire body. Jagged pain snaked up her spine, making her eyes water.

"Oh," she muttered, moving gingerly to discover the extent of the damage. Bruised, she decided, but there was nothing broken.

The side door she'd exited through burst open, pummeling the brick wall with a bang. Excited voices neared from behind, and she heard the rapid retreat of footsteps. Bother and damn. They'd escape before anyone could do anything. She had no idea what they looked like either, since they'd worn stocking ski masks to conceal their identities.

Asia clambered to her feet and dragged her aching body over to Roman. A nasty gash on his forehead and another on his left cheekbone marred the previous perfection of his features. Blood dripped down his face from a cut above his eyes, giving him a grotesque appearance. Asia checked his pulse. Still breathing, but he didn't seem conscious.

"Roman, can you hear me?"

Asia was aware that he shouldn't go to a hospital. The last thing any of them needed was a curious doctor or lab technician. The Resident Orcas would have a healer, the same as her tribe. Asia eased out a frustrated breath, wondering what to do. Damn, she couldn't take Roman to their healer, either. That would be more dangerous than the hospital.

A groan dragged her mind away from the dilemma. His eyes flickered.

"Roman," she whispered.

"What happened?" Frank crouched down beside them.

"Are you all right?" a cleaner asked, her wrinkled face pale with concern.

Roman struggled to sit, groaning even though Asia helped him.

"Someone attacked him," Asia said. "Roman, you okay? Do you want to go to the hospital?" She scooped up her handbag and pulled out an old serviette, which she pressed to the cut on his forehead.

"No. I'm fine." But he didn't sound like the Roman of earlier.

"I'll call the cops. And an ambulance," Frank added.

"No," Asia countered instinctively. On seeing Frank's incredulous look, she tried to make things right. "I don't think he needs an ambulance. I'll take care of him."

Judging by Frank's expression, she'd only succeeded in making things worse.

"What were they after? Do you think it was money?" the cleaner asked with avid curiosity.

Asia frowned at the question. "They didn't seem interested in stealing anything. Maybe it was drug related." The attack had seemed almost frenzied. Drugs were the only explanation that made sense.

"We'd better call the cops." Frank pulled his cell phone from his pocket.

Asia stayed him with a hand on his forearm. "It's late. I'll do it tomorrow morning, otherwise none of us will see our beds before daybreak." Asia pulled out a cell phone and pressed a speed-dial number. "Cab for Scarlet at the Blue Venetian Nightclub, please. Ten minutes? Great."

She closed the phone with a snap and glanced at Roman. His eyes were open and focused on her. "You okay? Do you think anything's broken?"

"I'm all right." He attempted to stand and wavered a fraction before Asia wrapped her arm around his waist to steady him.

Roman looked terrible with the blood on his face. In contrast, his cheeks were pale, and judging by his scrunched-up brow, his head ached. And his voice held a fraction of the self-assurance she'd noticed earlier.

Asia suppressed a snort. Kind of ironic, really. She'd wanted a hot date and all that might entail, but now it appeared as if she'd end up with babysitting duties.

"You'd better go and finish for the night," Frank told the cleaner. She nodded but turned away slowly, unwilling to miss any excitement. "I'll wait until the taxi arrives," Frank added.

Ten minutes later, as promised by the dispatcher, a white sedan pulled up outside the nightclub. Asia waved goodnight to Frank and climbed into the backseat with Roman. She found him another serviette and was relieved to see the blood flow had slowed.

They completed the fifteen-minute trip home to her Newmarket apartment in silence. Roman lay slumped in the corner of the cab, his eyes closed and his hand pressed to the wound on his forehead.

Asia cast him a worried look. Perhaps she should have risked a visit to the hospital. She leaned over to speak to the driver. "Just in front of the car parked up there."

The taxi pulled up where she indicated, and Asia handed the driver a credit card. With the payment taken care of, she turned to Roman. "You awake?" She gave his shoulder a gentle nudge and let out a sigh of relief when his eyes opened and he seemed more alert.

Roman yawned. "We home?"

"Yes." Asia grabbed her bag and slid from the cab, waiting to steady him if he needed her help. "I'm sure you'll feel better after a good night of sleep."

She hoped. If he didn't show signs of drastic improvement by tomorrow morning, she'd have to consider calling the Transients' healer, which would stir up trouble with a capital T.

A shudder worked through her body at the thought of the furor her announcement would bring, and she sent a prayer flying to the heavens. He did seem more alert.

Asia slipped her arm around his waist and led him to the entrance of the apartment block where she lived whenever she was in the city.

"My head's sore," Roman mumbled. "Tired."

"We'll have you in bed soon," Asia promised.

Mention of bed brought an entirely different scenario to her mind. Story of her life, she thought, shoving the vision from her head.

It refused to leave.

The play of muscles beneath her hand and his masculine scent undid all her resolutions to act as a Good Samaritan. The initial attraction she'd felt had strengthened into something consuming. Weird, considering she wasn't one to make snap judgments. According to her family, she was the original planner, and they didn't say that in a nice way. Asia admitted her penchant for plans and schedules. She considered things from all angles before coming to a decision, weighing the pros and cons. And there was nothing wrong with running her life in that way, even if her family thought differently.

"Here we are." Asia pulled away from Roman to rifle through her bag for her keys.

"You look very sexy tonight," he murmured, his smoky voice sending shivers of delight through her. "It's a pity I'm feeling so tired. Perhaps we can discuss how sexy you look again tomorrow morning?"

The keys slipped from her hands and landed on the tiled floor with a metallic clang. Asia stooped to retrieve them.

"What do you say? We on a promise?"

Asia felt her jaw go slack and hurriedly clamped her lips together. She hadn't heard wrong. "Um...okay." He'd forget his words by the morning.

After opening the door, she directed Roman inside. She flicked on the hall light, paused to lock the door, and guided him toward her bedroom. Asia concentrated on swallowing the nerves that leaped up from her stomach to combine in a knot at the back of her throat. Her tongue darted out to moisten her lips.

"I'm gonna shower before hitting the sack. Wash off this blood. Okay with you, sweetheart?"

"Um, sure." The idea of him naked in her shower pushed her libido a notch higher. This wasn't fair. He'd remember everything tomorrow and head back to his island kingdom without another word of sex or bed or anything resembling horizontal. That's if he deigned to speak to her. For some unfathomable reason, she wasn't concerned with her safety, because he didn't strike her as a bad man. She hoped she wasn't wrong.

"You going to shower with me?"

Asia felt herself blink. Oh man, temptation on two legs, but it wasn't right to take advantage of a man in this condition. "You need to sleep. If I shower with you, we'll get sidetracked."

Roman's dark gaze tracked down her body and back up to her face. A sexy smile—another of those panty-lowering ones—bloomed on his battered face. "That is true," he acknowledged. "Maybe you're right. It'll be quicker if I shower on my own." He slipped the ripped and bloody suit jacket off and let it drop to the floor.

When he started on the buttons of his shirt, Asia decided it was time to flee. "I'll grab you a clean towel." She shot from her bedroom as if a pack of Resident Orcas were after her. Her breathing had turned choppy, and her palms were moist. She felt as if she'd swum across the Tasman Sea from Australia to New Zealand in record time.

Asia wiped the dampness from her palms and took a deep breath. This couldn't continue. She was an adult, for goodness sake. With trembling hands, she tugged open the cupboard and seized several towels.

The pipes clanked, indicating Roman had found the shower and turned on the water. Just the image of his naked body made her break into a cold sweat. She scowled.

All she could think of was sex. The rush of pleasure at the moment of orgasm. Doing it with Roman.

Her steps slowed. She heard the shower door open and close and imagined his naked body. Muscled. Tanned. Very touchable.

Oh boy.

Asia fanned her flushed face. Sucking in a deep breath, she headed for the bathroom and temptation. "He's injured," she whispered. "You shouldn't be thinking about jumping his bones." *Besides, he's a sworn enemy of our tribe.*

Asia stepped into the bathroom, her gaze shooting to the shower. She could see his body without difficulty despite the fragrant steam filling the room. And it was just as spectacular as she'd imagined.

The water shut off, and the shower door opened. Asia thrust the towels at Roman, trying hard not to stare. It was all of two seconds before her resolve weakened and she sneaked a peek. Powerful shoulders gave way to a tight, trim waist and slim hips. Muscles. Oh yeah...muscles. Tight, toned, and sexy. Asia craved a touch. The trouble was that strangers had just pummeled him like a punching bag.

She shouldn't have sex on the brain. This crush she had on Roman Anderson was bad news. A quick roll between the sheets and a few hasty kisses were one thing, but this insidious craving for more had to stop before someone got hurt. *Before she got hurt.*

A relationship between members of opposing tribes was out of the question. Her family would disown her, and Asia freely admitted that would hurt. Despite their faults, she loved her mother, her brother, and sister, and couldn't imagine going through the rest of her life never seeing them. In isolation. A male wasn't worth that kind of sacrifice, not even a shifter who made her hot and needy.

"You're going to feel sore tomorrow," she said after catching his dark gaze on her face. Damn, that was masculine interest she saw in his eyes. This had to stop.

Now. Be strong.

"Maybe," he conceded, glancing down at his colored and bruised ribs in a disinterested manner. "I'm tired. Just want to sleep." He leaned closer to buzz a kiss across her lips before dropping the towel on the floor and sauntering back to the bedroom.

Asia gaped at his bare ass and at the wet buttercup-yellow towel on the bathroom floor. She didn't know which disturbed her most—the expanse of naked temptation or the fact that he expected her to pick up after him. Her astonishment turned to a scowl, and she kicked the towel out of her way. It hit the wall and settled, damp and taunting, in a soggy pile.

A groan from the bedroom had her sprinting to investigate. She arrived beside her queen-size bed to see Roman sprawled out, still buck-naked and looking very comfortable. Asia swallowed another attack of lust and pure craving. Her fingers itched to touch. The front view surpassed the rear one, she decided on a decadent sigh.

Jeepers, this was not fair.

How could she do the right thing when presented with this sort of temptation? Asia stepped a little closer. A soft chuckle jerked her gaze from his groin region.

"Hold that thought, babe." He gave a sleepy grin and closed his eyes. "Because I intend to collect on it tomorrow."

Asia stared, studying Roman with a combination of awe and astonishment. Desire. Oh yes, she desired him despite logic telling her that seeing Roman was a mistake and her acceptance of the problems a relationship between the two would bring.

She wanted him.

She craved, dammit!

A gentle snore erupted, interrupting her mental struggles about what was proper. At least he was sleeping peacefully. She'd send him on his way in the morning and put the whole sorry episode behind her.

Meanwhile, Roman Anderson was sleeping in her bed.

So much for her scratching a sexual itch.

Asia collected her sleep shirt from under the pillow on the other side of the bed, and with a last look at Roman, she headed for the spare bedroom.

The alarm went off way too early the next morning, but thoughts of Roman had kept her awake for what was left of the night. She'd tossed and turned until the bedclothes twisted in a helpless mess. Asia stumbled from the bed and slammed her palm on the alarm's off button. The piercing racket shut off, leaving blissful silence.

She cast a longing glance at the bed but dragged herself away, knowing she needed to check on Roman. Her steps quickened, and she burst into her bedroom.

Roman lay on his side with his back to her. Not a sound broke the silence in the bedroom, and alarm grew in Asia. She rushed to the bed, her heart thudding in sudden horror.

Was he dead? Had she screwed up by not taking him to the hospital?

She rounded the bed and leaned over him, straining to hear his breathing. He couldn't be dead. *He couldn't.* Asia imagined the kafuffle and shivered with a trace of fear. The man wasn't breathing. With a trembling hand, she reached out to touch his shoulder. Just as her hand touched his bare skin, he moved.

Asia let out a shriek and tried to jump clear.

"Morning, babe. I missed you." He held her fast despite her struggles and jerked her onto the bed.

Asia toppled against his naked chest, shock rendering her silent.

"Where have you been? I woke up and you weren't here."

Asia thumped him in the middle of the chest and immediately felt guilty when he winced. "Sorry. You gave me a fright. I thought you were dead."

"Nope. My ribs are sore and I have a headache. Apart from that, I feel fine." Roman nuzzled the soft skin of her neck and shifted slightly so their bodies aligned.

A shiver swept down her torso. She was acutely conscious of the fact that Roman was naked beneath the sheet, and all she wore was a thin cotton T-shirt. She wriggled uncomfortably.

"Babe, watch that squirming."

Asia was slow to understand until he took her hand and placed it firmly on his morning erection. The glint in his dark eyes confirmed the direction of his thoughts.

"Um, I don't think you...we should do this so soon after the assault."

"What's wrong with wanting to make love to my wife?" Roman demanded, and he kissed her, sealing her objections against his lips while his fingers strummed over the ruby and diamond band on her left hand.

Chapter Two

R oman Anderson thought they were married.

Married!

The word reverberated through her head while he continued to kiss her, nibbling at her lips until she gasped. He took immediate advantage, his tongue sliding inside her mouth, stroking, teasing, and generally making her crazy. He drew her closer still, kicking free of the sheet covering him and rolling so he pressed her into the mattress.

Her heart reveled in the weight of him. His scent—her soap from his early morning shower—drove her to give up her inner fight. Touch. She wanted to touch, and ignoring the voice of reason, she did. Trembling hands cupped his face and slid through his silky, dark hair. A moan built deep in her chest while her pulse rate accelerated.

Roman eased out of the kiss and drew back to smile down at her. "How did I ever luck out getting you to marry me?"

Asia swallowed. *Someone hit you on the head. If you were in your right mind, you wouldn't be here.* Guilt rose to nip her sharply in the conscience. She had to tell him the truth before the lie became too big. Already, it had taken on a life of its own.

Roman grinned. "Not going to answer? You never used to—" He broke off with a trace of confusion, his hands tightening on her shoulders. When he noticed her wince, he grimaced in apology and bent to soothe the ache with a kiss. "What's going on? Everything is blank. I don't recall how we met or our wedding day or anything." Roman removed his hands from her shoulders and sat up on the bed. He ran a hand through his thick hair. "Dammit, I don't know your name!"

Asia sat up and wrapped her arms around his

shuddering shoulders. "Shh. It's okay," she murmured. "Do you remember last night?"

She held her breath, awaiting his answer.

"I recall waking up on the ground in that alley," he said after a long silence. "But that's it."

His frustration was evident, but Asia wasn't about to tell him they were mortal enemies—their families and tribes. And she wasn't about to try to contact his family either. That would be suicide.

"It will be okay," she repeated. "Obviously, the thump on your head has affected your memory. Do you feel any pain? Should I take you to the hospital? You didn't want to go last night."

"I feel about as good as a man can expect after being jumped by a bunch of thugs. I don't think I like hospitals," Roman said, a scowl highlighting his words. "There's this sort of panicky sensation inside me when I hear the word."

Asia wasn't surprised. From the moment their mothers pushed them out of the deep water for their first breath, orca shifters had the need for secrecy emphasized for their safety. Fear of discovery kept their species alive in this modern world.

Roman's savage curse broke into her thoughts. "Damn, you'd think I'd remember my wife's name."

"Asia. My name is Asia."

He stared at her before nodding. "Yeah. Okay. That fits. Exotic and beautiful just like you. What happened to the hair?"

Oh shit. She'd forgotten about taking off the wig. She thanked her lucky stars again that she'd touched up the regrowth yesterday, so not a bit of the giveaway orca white showed at her temple. "I use the wig for my singing act."

"So I'm the only one who sees the real you," he said, his voice low and throaty and full of sexual promise.

A tingle sprang to life at her breasts. Her nipples puckered against the cotton of her T-shirt.

Roman reached out and traced the tip of one finger along the neckline. Asia's breath caught. The well-washed fabric stretched with ease. His finger dipped, traveling into bountiful cleavage.

"I think my wife is beautiful."

"But I'm not—"

Roman captured her denial against his lips, and she wasn't about to forgo the expertise of his mouth. She'd tell him later, she thought, her mind fogging and unable to think much past the man who seemed intent on having his wicked way.

"I think this should go." The first words he uttered when they came up for air.

Before she could voice a protest, he had the T-shirt

33

off and flying away. Asia watched with resignation as the cotton puddled into a pile in the middle of her bedroom carpet. The man had a proclivity for dropping things on the floor.

"Beautiful," he whispered. "God, how could I forget your perfection? Your breasts are beautiful." He cupped the creamy curves with his tanned hands and lifted one to his mouth. "Big, luscious and sexy. Just the way I like." His eyes drifted shut as he concentrated on taste and sensation.

Asia felt torn even as he licked her nipple and pulled her deeper under his sensual spell. She wanted to tell the truth but hated to end the pleasure his fingers and mouth set alight. Her teeth sank into the cushion of her bottom lip.

Damn, the man was a magician and they hadn't even reached the good part yet. She bit down harder. It sure as heck looked as if they were heading for the sexy stuff.

Maybe she'd tell him…later.

After all, they would have ended up in bed last night if the date had taken its course. Maybe. Probably, she acknowledged in a burst of honesty. Roman Anderson would be difficult to resist.

He sucked on her nipple, using his mouth and teeth. Small arrows of pain darted the length of her body, setting her on edge. Asia squirmed, and he lifted his head. His dark eyes glowed.

"Are you going to touch me? I'm sure I'd like that. Don't I?" The boyish uncertainty melted the last remnants of her guilt.

There was nothing wrong with having sex with a man. Asia pushed aside the fact their tribes were sworn enemies, deciding to enjoy the moment.

"Let's see, shall we?" She smiled when the apprehension melted from his eyes.

He lay back on the mattress and shifted until he was spread-eagled on the bed. "Do your worst."

Asia sat back on her heels to look her fill. The knowledge that he was watching her made her feel hot. Powerful.

"Don't make me wait too long. I'm ready now. Very ready," he added with a rueful glance at his cock.

"I can see that." Asia's gaze slid down his body to his erection. Long. Hard. Thick. He was set to go all right. She moved closer and bent over him to press a quick kiss to his lips. "Don't move an inch," she warned. One glance at his face told her the order amused him.

"What are you going to do?" His words confirmed the thought.

"Wait and see." She pinched his nipple hard enough to make him jump.

"Perhaps the gaps in my memory are a good thing. It's like we're making love for the first time. I noticed I don't have any clothes here in the bedroom. Are we separated?"

Oh boy. The lie just got better and better, growing like a certain puppet's nose. Yep, the hole she dug grew deep enough for her to jump right inside. "I—"

"Let's talk after. Please," he said. "I want to make love to you so bad. Whatever is in the past can stay there. This is a chance for a fresh beginning. For both of us." His hand snaked around her neck, tugging her off balance so she fell against his chest. He winced but held her tucked in place, despite his bruises and sore muscles.

Their lips met and mated in a slow kiss, sending shockwaves racing through her body. Roman took them deeper, making the kiss more aggressive. Hungry. Tongues dueled, thrusting and parrying in a harbinger of the consummation to come.

He rolled, his biddable and accepting self fading away, replaced by the alpha male who knew precisely what he wanted. Asia took the coward's way out and let him direct their loving. It wasn't difficult since his touch sent her soaring and wiped away her uncertainties.

He kissed down her neck and dallied at the hollow of her throat. His lips skirted her collarbone, gently biting then soothing the nip with a wet kiss.

Tormenting her. Each kiss, each love bite, drove her need higher until she wanted to demand he stroke her breasts, trail his hand along her cleft to find her swollen clit. The thought made her fidget. She needed his mouth, his fingers...

Asia cupped a breast with her hands, offering it to him. "Kiss my breast again," she whispered.

"With pleasure." His smoky voice slid across her nerve endings. Her pulse raced, and at the intimate juncture between her thighs, her body moistened, readying for his penetration.

He nuzzled her breasts, but this time didn't take her nipple into his mouth. No, this time he teased her until she wanted to beg for his talented caresses. His lips drifted lower, and he pressed kisses to her rib cage and her belly. Asia's breath stalled before an ache in her chest reminded her to breathe.

Roman moved down the bed and parted her legs. Shyness hit her for an instant until she remembered they were supposedly married. Grief, she'd never carry off this charade. Asia made a conscious effort to relax, and he made an approving sound deep in his throat.

"You're going to have to tell me what I did that's made you so wary," he whispered. "But not now. Let's concentrate on having fun and making each other feel good." He punctuated his disturbing and perceptive comments with more kisses. One on her abdomen. One on her hipbone. A kiss on her pelvic bone.

Asia's heart pumped out a few extra beats. She arched up in silent demand for a more intimate kiss. A chuckle sounded as he nipped the tender skin of her inner thigh. She jumped and steeled herself for another bite. Instead, he licked her inner thigh in ever-increasing circles, coming closer and closer to where she needed his touch most.

"Yes," she whispered. "No more teasing. Please."

"But it's so much fun playing with you." His warm breath puffed against her engorged nub.

A sharp spike of pleasure shot the length of her body.

"Your breathing changes, and you make these cute little whimpers at the back of your throat when I do something you particularly like." He tongued a delicate trail the length of her cleft, circling her aching clit but not touching enough to give her relief from the urgency attacking her senses.

"Yeah, that's it. Whimper for me again, babe." He licked again, but this time made a brief foray across her clit.

A shower of tingles burst to life, and she heard herself cry out but didn't feel the slightest bit of mortification. *Damn that felt good.* When he repeated the process, she waited until his tongue was almost there and jerked her hips upward. A bolt of sensation seared her with the extra contact.

"Yes," she moaned. "More."

Roman chuckled. "That was sneaky." He shifted away, putting more distance between them than Asia thought was necessary.

"I don't like teasing." Asia wanted to move things along because her conscience kept screaming at her. Once they'd done the deed, they couldn't stop. Halting right now before culmination was gonna kill her, but if he didn't hurry, her conscience was going to win out.

"Hmm." Roman smiled. "Close your eyes, babe."

"So you can tease me some more?"

"Go on. Close your beautiful eyes for me."

Asia stared at him for a long moment before obeying. She felt his hands on her hips and the dip of the mattress when he shifted positions.

"Are your eyes still closed?"

"Yes," Asia said, unable to keep the bite of impatience from her answer.

He laughed again, a short burst of humor before silence reigned. Asia heard her breathing, loud and choppy once again. She heard the faint tick of her alarm clock from where it sat on a dressing table on the far side of the bedroom. But she couldn't fathom what Roman was doing. She wasn't sure whether she should worry or not. So far, he hadn't done anything to alarm her, and nothing in his reputation concerned her either. Rumor said he'd had a few serious relationships and remained friends after parting. Asia strained to hear any noise to clue her in on what she could expect. Something sexy. Something pleasurable. She hoped. Her breasts ached. Nerves danced in her stomach while lower, a series of tiny pulses deep in her sex made her fidget. The fact her legs were parted, leaving her pussy open to his inspection intensified her arousal. She was wet and so ready for him. Why wasn't the dratted man hurrying?

"You're gorgeous," he whispered. "So easy to love you."

Asia's eyes flew open at his declaration. He stroked his hand the length of his cock, his dark gaze meeting hers. The flush of arousal in his eyes stole her breath. Then, before shock finished reverberating through her, he pinned her with his greater bulk, guided his cock to the mouth of her pussy and thrust inside.

The sudden penetration took her by surprise, and a gasp escaped as she struggled to take him. Roman hadn't used birth control. She froze, trapped in her lies. If they were married, it wouldn't matter, or he'd assume she was taking a form of birth control.

"Okay?" he demanded, holding himself in check for an instant.

Stretched to capacity, she could only nod and hold tight

to his shoulders.

His naked cock felt great, and she loved the fact there was nothing between them. The thought brought a surge of juices. The chances of her conceiving were low since orcas didn't breed often or easily. Diseases weren't a problem for them. She'd hope for the best and deal with the consequences later should the need arise.

He withdrew and drove back inside, her pussy clutching greedily this time. Roman repeated the move, stroking steadily until Asia shuddered. Their mouths met. Mated in a moist, erotic duel. Roman's cupped her butt with his hands and deepened the angle of penetration. Pleasure danced through her—heat and light. A sweet burn as their bodies rocked together. This was magical, sexual compatibility at its best, better than she'd ever imagined...

"Was it always this good?" he asked when their lips parted.

Asia trembled, each of Roman's strokes pushing her harder, closer to orgasm, even as guilt plagued her uneasy mind. But, she told herself, he felt the magic, so it wasn't all on her side.

He pulled back and slammed home with increasingly urgent hunger. Her hips jerked and she felt a tightening sensation deep in her pussy. The streaks of pleasure rushed together, converging in an immense explosion of sensation. He thrust into her again, then stilled. Asia felt the powerful jet of semen when he came and clasped him tighter, wrapping her arms around him because she didn't want to let go. When he finally relaxed, he rolled them both over and arranged her against his body. A man who liked to cuddle. Who'd have guessed? Asia gave a satisfied sigh and melted against his sweaty chest.

It was the best sex she'd ever had, and Asia didn't want to tell Roman the truth. She wanted to keep him forever.

CHAPTER THREE

"There is nothing familiar about the house at all?"
Asia finished showing Roman around the house
she owned north of Auckland on the wild west coast. She'd
decided to bring him to her territory rather than hang out
at the family apartment in the city.

The weird phone calls she'd received before they left
had sealed her decision. The last thing she needed was her
family or friends turning up to hurt him. She couldn't bear

it if her pretense ended with him hurt when he was the innocent party to this deception. Of course, they could look for her here, but she'd risk it. Mostly, they rang to let her know they intended to visit.

"Nothing at all." His terse voice pulled her out of stressing and dumped her deeper into guilt territory.

For all of two seconds.

Although Roman was frustrated with his memory loss, Asia wanted to screech her relief aloud. The pretend marriage could continue. She knew it was wrong—she did, but when would she have such an opportunity again? The chance to be herself with one of her own. They could swim off the coast together, hunt fish, and play in their killer whale forms. She'd only ever done that with her family. Swimming with a lover sounded like fun. A bolt of sheer lust swept through her. They could repeat this morning.

All day if they wanted.

Her body moistened when she imagined Roman possessing her again. And her doing things to Roman, touching him intimately, tasting him intimately. A shiver racked her body.

"Cold, babe?"

"Not exactly." The amusement in his dark gaze made her look away with another surge of guilt. She was doing the right thing, wasn't she? Of course, she was, since a nagging instinct told her that the weird phone calls had something to do with the attack on Roman. She didn't like the idea they'd followed them to her apartment, but it was possible.

"Why don't you want to go to the doctor?" she asked, deciding it would seem strange if she didn't push. The lump on the back of his head was huge, though it didn't seem to slow him down.

"I don't know." Roman paced past her to the window. He pushed aside the creamy net curtain to stare outside and let it fall back into place. He walked to the dresser and plucked a silver-backed hairbrush off the top. Thumping it down again, he turned to face her with a scowl. "I can't explain. I don't understand it, but the thought of visiting a doctor fills me with fear." He flashed a crooked grin that charmed Asia and made her want to smother him with kisses. "Bet you didn't know your husband was so weird."

"I did actually." Asia sauntered toward him, not stopping until her arms linked around his neck. She grinned up at him and ruffled his dark curls, taking care to avoid the knot on the back of his head. "That's part of why I love you. Your charm."

A dark brow rose. "That it?"

"And your expertise in bed," Asia added. As she watched, his other eyebrow rose, and her mouth dropped open in awe. "I wish I could do that. My eyebrows don't work independently."

"It's a gift. We can make love any time you want. Any time. Any place and I'm yours. You should know that, babe," he said in a chiding voice.

"We have time this week to do whatever you want." Asia pushed aside the ramifications of him regaining his memory. Instinctively, she knew it would return. No doubt he'd never speak to her...or worse, it could cause further trouble between tribes. Asia was determined to make it clear she was the one at fault. Asia didn't care about a personal backlash. She'd made her bed and, by heck, she wanted to lie in it.

"Do you know what I'd like most of all?"

"Judging by the serious look on your face, I'd say it's not sex, more's the pity." Asia smoothed her fingers across his wrinkled brow. "Is your head aching?"

"A bit. I'm fine." He shrugged off her concern and stepped out of reach, telling Asia without words that he was tired of her fussing. "I'd like to go for a walk along the beach. I think I like the sea and swimming."

Roman wondered at the sharp look Asia narrowed on him. Part astonishment and part shock. It made him wonder if he'd done the right thing in not asking more questions about their life together.

"A walk sounds great." She avoided his gaze again.

Roman stood back and let Asia precede him. What the hell had happened to blow their relationship apart? It had nothing to do with sex because they communicated perfectly in that sphere. Roman's rueful grin lit on Asia's curvy butt. Any more perfect and he'd have trouble walking. At least they were working on putting things right. They'd been together during his attack, which meant they were still talking, trying to find common ground and forge a future together. He liked the thought of growing old with a sexy woman like Asia.

They walked out the front door, down two steps, and were on the beach.

Asia paused to remove her shoes and chucked them up near the door. Roman did likewise, relishing the heat of the black sand under his feet. He reached for Asia's hand and tugged her closer, the salty tang in the air relaxing the tight pressure banding his chest. Overhead, a lone gull rode the air currents while the crash of the breakers as they raced to shore relaxed him. The coil of tension released even further.

"Do I like the water?" A gut instinct told him he loved swimming, but he wanted confirmation.

A gamine grin flashed. "That's what I like about the

house. The sea and the privacy." She stopped walking and started undressing.

Roman gawked then smirked as she revealed her body piece by piece with the finesse of a professional stripper. A cotton shirt. A lacy bra. Denim shorts. Pink cotton panties.

"Last one in is a rotten egg." Asia sprinted down the beach, leaving him standing above the watermark, still staring. It was hard not to ogle his wife. Tall and curvy enough that he felt safe holding her tight. He didn't worry about squashing her or crushing a rib. Roman's gaze wandered down her back and lingered at her trim waist before he started to strip.

Damn, he was a lucky man.

He shucked his clothes, leaving them in an untidy heap, and hurried into the surf. The water was cool against his heated skin. This had been a good idea.

Already, the aching at his temples had ceased. He cut through the water, diving through the waves when they approached, steadily gaining on Asia. He heard her laugh above the roar of the surf and grinned. Oh yeah. He liked the water all right, but making love to his wife would take priority. She couldn't flaunt her luscious body at him without reprisals. He lunged and she evaded him, stopping a few feet away to grin.

"Headache gone?" she asked.

"Yeah, it has. How did you know?" Roman realized his headache had vanished, and he felt great. Invigorated. He swam a few lazy strokes until he was close enough to touch her. The sun shone down from overhead, a soft breeze blew, and Asia treaded water right next to him. Roman slid his arms around her neck and drew her flush with his naked body. The sun caught the water droplets on her face, making her sparkle. He felt pressure around his heart as though a fist squeezed it tight. A lump formed in his throat. Roman swallowed and lowered his head to taste her passion.

Their lips moved together leisurely as if they had all the time in the world.

Asia pulled away to survey him intently. "Do you feel an urge?"

"Always," he replied, smirking. "I want to slide deep into your pussy and love you until you scream."

She swallowed, and an expression that might have been panic or something else flitted across her face. "I'd like that too, but that's not what I meant."

A wave knocked them together, their bodies jostling until it passed and continued its journey to shore. His erection brushed her abdomen, and he squeezed his eyes shut to enjoy the teasing sensation. The promise of what would come when they loved each other. Suddenly, his skin prickled. A warning? Or something else. His eyes snapped open to see Asia studying him intently, as if she knew something he didn't.

"Watch me," she said. "Hold the image you see in your mind, and the change should occur. I hope." Asia pulled away from him, leaving him in confusion. Image?

What the hell was she talking about? Roman groped for understanding, knowing from her serious expression he'd missed something important.

"I don't—" He broke off, his eyes widening in shock. The air around her shimmered, and it had nothing to do with the glint of the sun. It was Asia. As he stared, her face lengthened. She transformed before his eyes into a sleek black and white fish. Long and streamlined with a dorsal fin.

"Holy shit." That was no fish. She'd turned into a killer whale in front of his eyes.

Asia swam around him in a tight circle before backing away and poking her head and flippers from the water. Then she sank out of sight. Spy-hopping. He dredged the word from his befuddled mind. What did she mean hold the image?

Roman scowled. He might like swimming, but he wasn't a damn whale. Was that why she'd acted so uneasy earlier on, when her behavior and actions didn't fit? Because she'd hoped to hide their differences? A hollow feeling punched him in the gut.

He was married to a fish.

The whale—Asia—swam closer, and if an orca could frown, that's what she was doing. She nudged him roughly in the chest, hard enough to make him go under the water. When he came up spluttering, she waited for him. Her mouth gaped open, revealing large white teeth that curved backward to her throat. Asia pulled away and rolled suddenly onto her side. She slapped her fin on the surface of the water.

One. Twice. Three times. Salt water smacked Roman in the face, and a rogue wave surprised him. He came up gasping for air and pissed off.

"That's enough." Roman turned away from Asia and swam strongly, catching a wave and body surfing to shore. He turned his head to see Asia keeping pace with him without even trying. Stumbling to his feet, he waded from the water, desperate for some peace and time to come to terms with his discovery. Splashing beside him attracted his attention.

"Go away." He couldn't speak any blunter than that.

Worry knotted Asia's throat, jamming up words of denial.

He was looking at her as if she were some kind of monster. Panic, like she'd never felt before, sapped her strength. She shifted back to human form even as she glided onto the sandy beach. The usual pleasure she derived from the ocean seeped away, leaving a yawning, aching throb in her chest and at the back of her eyes. This was her punishment for lying to Roman. She'd been sure that instinct would take over once he'd immersed himself in the water.

It hadn't.

To put it simply, she was screwed.

And she had no idea what to do to make everything right.

"Roman." Asia hated the pleading note in her voice. One lay and a few kisses, and she was thinking permanent.

How sad was that?

The ache at the back of her eyes intensified.

"I don't want to speak to you." He presented her with his back and strode away.

Sudden fury whipped through Asia. He was not going to pull that crap on her. He could talk to her whether he wanted to or not. She ran after him and grabbed his shoulder. He attempted to shrug her off, but she persisted until he whirled to face her.

"What?"

"I'm not a monster."

"No, you're a freak. *A fish.*"

Asia let rip before she thought things through. Her bunched fist connected with his jaw, snapping his head back.

"I am an orca," she gritted out. "I eat fish."

She glared at him. Her chest heaved—her naked chest—and she decided arguing naked in the middle of the beach, even though it was private, was not the wisest course.

"Fine," she snapped. "We can talk about it later, but you might like to know you're a shifter too." His face paled, and Asia took great satisfaction from his reaction for a fleeting instant. Shame crept in on the heels of her silent gloating.

Roman's mouth worked. He swallowed. "I don't believe it." Underlying the words, she heard a trace of panic. He doubted her—it showed in his face, and as she watched, anger boiled up to cope with his confusion. "I am *not* a fish."

"No, you're a great big bloody stubborn whale." She threw up her hands like a drama queen and flounced back into the ocean.

Fine. Let him think that.

She'd give him space to cool off and take time out herself. Asia checked the vicinity for prying eyes, then smoothly

53

shifted and dived into the cool ocean. She swam at high speed, sending schools of startled fish flitting away in terror. The need to breathe forced her to the surface. Asia drove upward, leaping clear of the water in a graceful breach.

She landed in the water with a mighty splash and swam hard and fast again, trying to outrun her frenzied thoughts. Would Roman accept her word? Would he even still be there when she returned to her house?

Three hours later, invigorated and at peace with herself, she returned to the beach and her house. She'd concluded she couldn't force Roman to acknowledge his heritage. Acceptance needed to come from him.

Asia ambled up the beach, aware of trepidation despite her decision. Making love with Roman had awoken feminine needs long suppressed. Despite what the rest of her family thought, she'd always thought Roman Anderson looked like a good man.

Now she knew it firsthand. The man possessed humor and goodness. The great body didn't hurt either. She sighed. Unfortunately, the long-held crush had turned into a stronger emotion...

She walked up to where she'd left her clothes. They were gone. Asia kicked at a pile of sand. Childish. Stupid. All because she'd told him the truth. She stomped up the footpath and wrenched the door open.

"Roman?" She slammed the door and stormed through the open-plan living area to the kitchen. "Roman!" He'd left. Figured.

"In here," a masculine voice called.

Asia halted. "Roman?"

"In the bedroom."

Asia reached her bedroom in three large steps. She stood in the doorway and stared at the naked male, relaxed and at ease with his unclothed state.

"I'm sorry. I still don't remember anything, but I decided you wouldn't lie to me. Not about this."

"Thanks." Asia leaned against the doorjamb, trying not to focus on the family jewels. "I think."

A slow grin crept across his face. He'd noticed precisely where she was looking.

"Wanna make up?" His dark brows waggled up and down. "How about it?"

"On one condition."

"Which is?"

"That you never call me a fish again." Asia folded her arms over her chest and met his gaze with a challenging one of her own. "Well?"

"Fair enough, since you insist I'm one too."

Asia straightened and padded over to the bed. An arm

snaked out, jerking her off balance. She landed with a soft *oomph*. He held her firmly, aligning their bodies until she felt every inch of him caressing her body. Roman rolled without warning, grinning down at her.

"You're an orca, the same as me. That's part of why I didn't push you about seeking medical treatment. We can't see doctors in case our differences are noted. None of us wants to be treated like lab rats."

Roman traced his fingers across one breast, following the delicate network of veins beneath her skin. His eyes were dark and serious when he looked at her again. "I can understand shapeshifters wanting to maintain secrecy. Do you think my conditioning kicked in and I instinctively refused medical attention?"

"Yeah. I do."

"Why were we separated? Was there someone else involved? I noticed all my clothes are in the other bedroom."

And the questions became harder and more challenging, the lie tightening around her neck like a noose. The clothes belonged to family members, and some wouldn't fit him. "I..." Asia shrugged helplessly, her stomach bucking up and down with nerves. The truth. She needed to tell him the truth. "We aren't—"

Roman's hand covered her mouth. "Wait. Let's take

this situation as a second chance. Maybe that's why it's happened. An omen."

Asia's breath eased out against the palm of his hand. Relief shot through her.

A second chance. Stupidly, she nodded when she knew nothing good could come of taking the pretense further. Sooner or later, Roman would regain his memory and find himself in bed with the enemy.

"Good. We're decided." He removed his hand and pressed his lips to hers. Slowly, he pulled away. "No more discussions about f...ah, whales. We'll make love instead." Roman licked the column of her throat. Her heart went pitter-patter, knocking so hard against her ribs it was a wonder Roman didn't hear and speculate about the cause. "I'm going to make love to you with my mouth. I'm going to taste you and love you until you scream."

Something deep within her belly fluttered. Her pulse quickened when she allowed herself to imagine his words becoming fact.

"You taste like the sea. Salty. Sexy." With each husky word, he moved until his face was level with her breasts. The coral-colored nipples puckered as they both watched. Asia bit back a groan. The man made her so hot, so needy.

He pinched one nipple. A sharp shard of pain-pleasure ripped the length of her body. Her pussy dampened in reaction. Another pinch made her moan. She'd never liked pain before, but with Roman, it was different.

His tongue darted out to bathe the slight nip he'd inflicted. She ached for the suction of his mouth, the sting of his teeth again.

"Please," she whispered in a thick voice she barely recognized.

"I don't suppose we have any toys hidden away in the drawers or the depths of the wardrobe?" He punctuated his words with a tweak at the underside of one plump breast.

"Toys?" Asia stared, shock and curiosity warring. "We haven't tried anything like that before," she finally ventured.

Roman frowned. "No? I could have sworn we—never mind. Hold that idea. We can improvise." He stood and gazed down at her with hooded eyes. "Part your legs for me. Yeah, just like that. Now touch yourself."

Shock—one piled on top of another. Did he...? Yeah, he did. And he'd think it strange if she didn't go along with his wishes. Especially as it seemed the depths of his memory were providing him with sexual history, both likes and dislikes. Asia slid her hand across her belly.

The corners of his mouth lifted in approval. "Show me what you like."

Asia's eyes slid to half-mast as her hand crept across her smooth pelvic bone and lower still.

"Keep your eyes open and on me," he ordered. "I want to see your beautiful eyes."

Her heart thundered as her finger slid down between her legs, dragging lightly on wet feminine flesh. Roman's eyes on her, watching her every reaction, intensified the rush of pleasure. A gush of arousal flooded her pussy. Her finger slid across slippery folds and circled her swollen clitoris.

"That's it," he whispered. "Keep going but don't let yourself come. Can you do that for me?"

Desire, strong and powerful, throbbed through Asia. Her finger circled her clit. She teased and stoked the fires inside higher. At the back of her mind, she heard footsteps when Roman left the bedroom. A shiver ran through her. She thrust her hips upward, working her finger and hips in countermoves.

Roman returned and put a cup on the stand beside the bed. "That's good, babe. How do you feel?"

"Empty," Asia said in a thick voice, wondering about the contents yet too submerged in satisfaction to care enough to peek.

"I can fix that for you, babe. Take your hand away now. Let me tend to you."

Asia heard herself gasp. Touching herself in front of

Roman had lit the fuse to passion and need that she'd never felt before. "Please," she whispered. He could do anything he wanted as long as he made her come.

Roman touched her flesh. Lightly. So softly, she wasn't certain. Then he touched her again and she was sure. A tremble swept through her. Hot. So hot. Her pussy clenched tight, and Asia bit down hard on her bottom lip, feeling as though she were poised on the edge of a cliff and would topple at the slightest push. Her eyes closed and the coiling tension intensified.

Something rattled. She heard a crunching sound. The mattress depressed and he settled between her legs. A puff of air breezed across her sensitive folds then she felt his mouth. An icy sensation hit, the contrast between hot and cold making her gasp. His cold tongue stroked along her slit, circled her nub.

An ice cube.

The rattle sounded again, and this time she knew what to expect. The piece of ice he stroked over her inner thigh still made her jump though. He alternated the playful strokes of the melting cube with his warmer tongue, moving closer to where she needed his touch.

"How does that feel?"

"Weird. Good." Her breath hitched when he sucked lightly on her clit. His lips were cold but his tongue and the interior of his mouth were hot. It drove her crazy, made her beg, something she'd never imagined herself doing with a man. "Please. Roman, please. More."

Roman backed off a bit, teasing her with delicate strokes, nibbles and the scrape of teeth. The little pinches brought another sensation, another layer to his seduction.

Her chest rose and fell, and she tried to anticipate where or when he would touch her next. His fingers. His mouth. Lord, she hoped he'd use his lips again. Just the thought of him kissing her intimately made her sex clench hard.

As if he sensed she was close, too close, he stopped tormenting her. A finger dragged the length of her cleft and thrust inside her needy body. Chills raced across her flesh at the invasion. She wanted to come so badly, yet contrarily, she wanted to string out the sensual experience and make it last.

"That's it, babe. Relax," he whispered in a voice that would tempt an angel. Asia was no angel.

Then she felt the hot touch of his tongue, dragging across her swollen flesh. He soothed the ache before tempting her higher, flailing her achy clit with his tongue, sucking gently with his mouth. The whole time he kept up a lazy thrust and withdrawal of his finger. Roman added another finger, stretching her until she felt pleasantly full. Pleasure coursed through her body, swirling and lifting her higher and higher until it swamped her. One final delicate lick pushed her into orgasm. She gasped, convulsing, her vagina clamping down on his fingers for long, decadent moments.

Asia's eyes fluttered open to find Roman grinning up at her.

"Again," she whispered.

Immediately, her pussy clenched.

"Good," he said, withdrawing his fingers. He slid up her body and kissed her hard, passion sparking between them. She tasted herself on him when his tongue delved deep into her mouth. His heavy thigh pushed between her legs until she parted them even wider. With one quick stroke, he surged inside her tight sheath. She shuddered at the full sensation, enjoying the way he took her with such confidence. He made her feel needed. Feminine.

His possession was so good.

Perfect.

He stroked strongly, brushing against her engorged flesh, driving her high again into a place where sensation ruled. And just like that, Asia toppled head over heels and irrevocably in love with her enemy.

CHAPTER FOUR

"I'd like to go swimming again." Roman nuzzled her neck and blew a light stream of warm air into her ear.

"That tickles." Asia tried to squirm away, but her limbs refused to obey. Her entire body felt like builder's putty. The days since their arrival had slipped away, full of loving and togetherness. Roman hadn't regained his memory or the ability to shift.

Asia tried not to worry, concentrating on loving him, but the future was like a ticking bomb with her caught in the explosion zone.

"A swim," he persisted.

Asia lifted her arm enough to check the time. A groan emerged. "It's the middle of the night."

"Then no one will see us," he countered, blowing again across the whorls of her ear. "I want you to explain to me how you shift. What do you do to start the process?"

"The beach is private. We don't have many visitors." Asia studied him closely, unable to demur or argue, not after their incredible days together. She inhaled, trying to decide how to handle his questions. It wasn't easy deciding when the scent of their loving filled the room, reminding Asia of her treachery. "My mother told me it's different for every shapeshifter. Changing forms isn't instinctive." Asia frowned. "Maybe that's why you're having trouble. You're trying too hard."

"Are you sure I'm an orca?" His gaze was intent, demanding answers.

"Oh yeah. I'm sure." Asia had seen him in person, seen him changing and flirting with female killer whales from his tribe while they swam together through the Cook Strait. She'd hidden, scarcely breathing or moving in case they sighted her.

"I thought the shifting thing might have been the problem between us." Roman tucked a lock of hair away from her face, his eyes holding questions that begged answers.

Asia didn't want to respond. A quick glance at his face told her she had to say something. He'd thought about their relationship during the last few days. "No," she said, relieved she could utter the truth, even if lies layered the facts.

"A third party?"

"No!"

"I didn't think so." Smugness coated his words. "We're too hungry for each other."

Because it was new, Asia thought, though it had never been like this with another male, either orca or human. Bother. She wished he'd quit with his questions.

Diversion. *Now.* "When I want to shift, I picture an orca in my mind and hold the image there. The change happens naturally as long as I hold the picture in my mind. When I want to shift back, I picture my human image. It's hard to explain."

"Sounds easy enough." Roman shrugged. "I think I should contact my family. I do have a family?"

Asia swallowed her alarm and wished the ground would do the same to her. How the heck did she sidestep this? His family would eat her for breakfast.

"Yes," she said, striving for a casual manner.

The Transient tribe told the young calves horror stories about the Resident rebels to keep them in line. Asia shuddered. Honestly, she thought the legends held enough truth to worry about the repercussions of crossing the Resident tribe.

"They're away on holiday. I thought about trying to contact them up in the islands, but they're keeping to orca form, which makes things difficult. Difficult for cell phones to work underwater. And your mother hasn't been well. I didn't want to worry her needlessly." Asia scrutinized him as the lies slipped glibly off her tongue.

He frowned, lines bracketing his sexy mouth before they smoothed away. "You're right, babe. I wouldn't want to worry my family."

Asia relaxed a fraction and offered him a tentative smile. Crisis averted, at least for the moment. Gossip told her that Roman's mother still lived. His father had died some time ago. Asia knew he had at least one younger brother but didn't know names or anything else about them. She needed to divert him. "I've been thinking. It's better to let you regain your memories naturally rather than me filling the gaps for you."

"But you'll help me with the shifting." He made it a

statement.

"You've worn me out. I need to sleep."

"We're not going to rest if we stay here. I want you again." He took her hand and placed it on his erect penis. Her fingers wrapped around his cock instinctively.

"You're definitely an orca." She sent him a rueful grin. "Orcas like sex."

"That a fact?"

"Yeah." Asia bent toward him and bit one pectoral muscle. At his mock growl, she jumped out of reach and winced at the protest of well-used muscles. "Perhaps swimming isn't such a bad idea. Might unkink my muscles."

Concern shaded his face, and he rapidly closed the distance between them. "Was I too rough?"

Asia ran her hand across his broad chest. The skin was warm beneath her fingers and tempting. She wanted to bite again but refrained. This time. "Nothing a good massage wouldn't cure," she said, her tone teasing.

The ring of the phone cut through the throbbing atmosphere that had sprung up between them.

Asia glanced away and couldn't prevent the stain of heat filling her cheeks. They'd made love several times, and all she could think of was more. "Ah, I'd better get that. It's probably my agent."

"This late?"

"You'd have to know my agent to understand."

The phone rang again, and Asia hurried to answer. "Mark, isn't it a bit late to ring?"

"*Secrets*," a voice whispered.

"I think you have the wrong number." Asia grimaced at Roman.

"*You have secrets*," the voice repeated. She had no idea if it was a male or female. "Secrets have a way of coming out when you least expect."

"I don't know what you're talking about. You have the wrong number." Asia dropped the phone back in the cradle, shoving aside the insidious fear crawling through her veins. "I'll go swimming if you give me a massage when we get back. And bring me breakfast in bed tomorrow morning." She smiled, trying to act naturally. Had it been a wrong number, or did someone know something about Roman? She willed the phone not to ring again, and when it didn't, her alarm faded. Coincidence. Sheer coincidence, she tried to tell herself.

It didn't work.

"I think I could arrange breakfast in bed. And a massage." Pure sex and lust sparkled in his dark eyes.

For an instant, she was tempted to seduce him immediately. But then Asia considered the phone calls she'd received before they left the Auckland apartment to drive north. Hang-ups. Not one but two. Alone, they were nothing distressing. Taken together with Roman's attack, they were more ominous, especially since they'd started here. Someone knew and was biding their time.

"Okay, you've talked me into a swim." She held out her hand. "Let's go."

Fingers clasped, they walked out the door and down the footpath leading to the beach. The sky was a deep, inky blue-black, and the moon peeked from behind a bank of clouds. It was as if they were the sole beings in existence. The mournful cry of a morepork rang out, piercing her complacency. Orca legend said the owl-like creature's warning meant bad luck would come.

Asia shivered with a chill, the hair prickling at the back of her neck. Commonsense told her the cry came from a nocturnal predator intent on finding his evening meal, but uneasiness still made her jumpy. The situation with Roman was running out of control, and each day, each minute, she felt herself drawn deeper into the lie.

"What happens if I can never change to an orca again?" Roman stopped and placed his hands on her bare shoulders. A crease marred the perfection of his brow. "Will you still love me if we can't swim together?"

Asia stared, a knot of shame and apprehension clogging

69

her throat and preventing her from replying straight away. She cleared the obstruction with a sharp cough.

"Of course I will." Her voice emerged not much louder than a whisper.

"That's good," Roman said, "because I don't mind admitting I'm worried. I keep trying to remember what it's like to swim as an orca. It's a foreign concept. I can't remember a damn thing about shifting." His hands clenched around her shoulders, his fingers digging painfully into her flesh.

"Big, bad Roman Anderson frightened?" Asia winked and attempted to lighten the moment by teasing.

"Yeah," he muttered. "Stupid, huh? But you tell anyone and I'll deny everything. Friends and family." He exhaled loudly, the sound telling her of his anguish at his loss of memory. Her stomach roiled with shame. Friends. She hadn't thought of friends looking for him. Family, yes, but not friends. If she told him the truth, would it help? Roman's hands dropped away, leaving her bereft. Asia sighed. In truth, she doubted her actions would differ if she had the time over again. Not when she'd lusted after him for so long. And now she loved him.

What a mess.

"I'm sure you'll rediscover how to shift forms soon. And remember your family. Your friends. Maybe not tonight, but soon." Asia wished she had the guts to take him to the Transient's healer. But the healer was an old man who should have been an old woman, given his love for gossip. She couldn't take the risk. While there hadn't been any bloodshed between the tribes for years, they didn't speak or acknowledge each other. Currents ran deep between the tribes, and it wouldn't take much to make the old animosity spill over into turmoil.

Asia battled the fractured thoughts of right and wrong, her guilt growing. One fact remained. If she told him the truth and returned him to his family, would she remain safe? She frowned. Was that the reason for the phone calls? Asia shied from her turbulent thoughts to concentrate on the present.

They crossed the expanse of black sand and paused at the water's edge.

Roman reached for her hand again, and she squeezed it lightly, offering him a reassuring smile.

"Give me a kiss for luck."

"As long as you don't get distracted."

"I could." Roman directed her hand to his straining erection, his white teeth flashing in a smirk. "But just a kiss this time." He sobered. "I want to do this."

A wave swirled around their ankles while they embraced, their lips clinging together. Asia let her eyes drift closed and savored his warmth and the feel of his strength when he pressed against her softer curves. An ache started at the back of her eyes. She gripped his biceps tighter and hung on, wishing that reality would never intrude. But she had to face this and help him.

They parted and turned to the open sea, walking into the cool water until they were waist deep.

"Picture a whale in your mind. Imagine the sleek black and white body, the large dorsal fin, the flippers, and the fluke."

"Shift. Don't wait for me." He sounded almost angry.

Asia forgave him his testy tone and merely nodded. She waded a short distance from Roman and transformed smoothly into orca form. As always, a rush of pleasure swept through her mind. She dived beneath the water, using her strong fluke to propel her along. After speeding out to sea for a few minutes, Asia circled back to where she'd left Roman. She cut through the water, keeping below the surface, swimming silently so she didn't disturb his concentration.

Please let him manage to shift, she thought, willing him to success.

Nothing happened.

Asia waited a little longer before approaching Roman and nudging him on the arm. When he ignored her, she prodded him again, careful to temper the move so she didn't hurt him with her superior strength.

He ran his palm across her back in a long, luxurious stroke. The man had magic fingers, knowing just how to touch her in either form. Her mind hazed with the pleasure of his hands on her flesh. Maybe she could pay for his services at a later date, or perhaps she should simply kidnap him and never let him go. Yeah, sounded like a plan.

"I can't change," he said. "I might as well go back to the house. You stay out here and enjoy the swim."

Asia heard the frustration and irritation underlying his words. There was no way she intended to leave him alone to brood. She moved closer, knocking him off balance. Another push sent him under the water.

He came up spluttering. "Dammit, Asia. Cut that out."

She maneuvered next to him, forcing him to grab hold of her to maintain his balance. When she felt his hand grasping her upright dorsal fin, she swam out to sea before he had a chance to let go.

"What are you doing?" Roman sounded grumpy but unalarmed. Asia kept swimming, taking care not to sink too far beneath the surface of the water. Roman needed air to breathe in his human form, but she wanted him to enjoy the surge of exhilaration when they raced through the water.

Asia knew exactly when the anger left him. His tight grasp on her dorsal released, and the grip of his knees around her body relaxed. She heard his laugh before the wind ripped it away. Smiling inside, Asia slowed, traveling more leisurely now that Roman had calmed. Love for this man swelled inside her. She wished she could reassure him his ability to shift would return. It wasn't as if he'd hit his head that hard. The swelling had almost disappeared, and the bump was no longer tender.

"This is beautiful, Asia." Roman smoothed his hand across her back in a firm and pleasurable caress. She shuddered, her heart beating faster from his proximity rather than the exertion of the swim. She cut through the inky water, the romantic in her enjoying the glint of the moonlight on the waves. It would be so good to swim with her lover in their true forms. Loneliness would never haunt her again with this orca by her side.

A series of deep clicks reverberated through the water, striking fear in Asia's heart. She slowed and listened carefully. There! A pod of whales singing to each other in a similar dialect to the one the Transients used. *Strangers.* Asia turned and headed back toward the shore, increasing her speed. Had Roman heard? Had he understood? Anxiety circled her mind.

Was it Roman's family? Asia feared her worst nightmare

was about to come true.

She'd die at the hands of the Resident Orcas. And once Roman heard the truth, he'd probably stand back to watch the carnage.

Asia hustled to shore, using the lights they'd left burning in the house as a guide. Fear of discovery stopped her from vocalizing for directional guidance. She kept swimming until she felt the brush of sand beneath her belly and shifted with Roman still riding her back. They landed at the water's edge in a tangle of limbs. Reacting with pure adrenaline, Asia grabbed for Roman and tugged his face down for a kiss. Lips slammed together, tongues dueled, noses bumped. It wasn't pretty, but she forced everything she felt for Roman into her kiss. Breathing heavily, they pulled apart.

A lazy grin tugged at his lips. "What was that for?"

"I love you." Asia cupped his face and stared into his eyes. "No matter what, remember that."

Roman frowned. "Hey, I'm not going to leave you."

Asia gulped. The truth. She was going to tell him right now. She couldn't live with the guilt a minute longer. "I haven't told you the whole truth."

Roman's frown intensified, and Asia rushed into speech before she chickened out. "We come from different tribes. Our families are bitter enemies." Her heart pounded anxiously while she waited for his reaction. They were both still naked and lying with their limbs entangled. Her breasts brushed his chest with each uneasy breath.

"Enemies." Roman studied her intently, watching, measuring her every reaction.

This was it, Asia thought. Regret for what might have been filled her, and tears backed up behind her eyes. She blinked. "Yeah." It was all she could manage in the way of a reply.

"I guess that's why the family hasn't come around to see us. Are we disowned?"

"Not exactly." Asia averted her gaze. She couldn't handle looking at him for much longer. The weight of culpability on her chest felt like suffocation. How did she justify her deception? No matter what words she spun, she was going to lose him.

"Explain," he said tersely.

"We're not married."

CHAPTER FIVE

Not married?

Nothing she could have said would have shocked him more. The ring she wore all the time—he'd thought it was a wedding ring.

Their wedding ring.

Roman started to speak before snapping his mouth shut. Anger built, pressing against his chest, words cramming up his throat until he thought he would explode. Why the hell had she lied?

"Why?" he gritted out finally.

"I don't know." She shrugged, a helpless grimace on her face. "It's all so complicated."

"We have time. Explain."

Asia pushed him away and sat up. She glanced at him uneasily as if she were suddenly uncomfortable with her nudity. Too damn bad. She wasn't leaving until she explained her mind games.

She wrapped her arms around her chest and eyed him warily. As he watched, she swallowed. Roman hardened his heart to her misery. She'd lied. Asia was the culprit here, and he wasn't about to let her off without an explanation.

"Well?" Roman attempted to rein in his temper. He didn't want her to sulk like his brother—

His brother.

He'd remembered one of his family members. Excitement kept him quiet while he concentrated, trying to grasp the foggy recollections dancing through his mind. The misty images dissolved the instant he tried to seize them.

"I...I've seen you in the papers, in the gossip pages, and at functions," Asia said in a low voice. "I've always admired you, but because of the feud between our families and tribes, there was no way we could meet socially." Asia darted a glance at him before looking away.

Roman kept his face passive and waited for her to continue. She'd lied to him. He couldn't get past that. Roman didn't think he liked lies.

"You came into the nightclub where I work as a singer. You asked me out for a date, and I agreed."

"Didn't I recognize you?"

She shook her head, her shoulders drooping in abject misery. Roman had the absurd need to draw her into his arms and hold her, to soothe away her uneasiness with a kiss. Or two.

"No. It's not surprising. I've spent a lot of time overseas and keep a fairly low profile, so I wouldn't expect you to know me."

"Go on."

"When I went to meet you outside the club, I found three men attacking you. They ran off when I called for help. You hit your head on the pavement. When you regained consciousness, you thought I was your wife. I tried to tell you but...but you had other things on your mind."

Like sex. Roman grimaced. What red-blooded male wouldn't think of sex when confronted by Asia's voluptuous curves? He replayed the last few days, trying to remember Asia's reactions to his questions. She had tried to talk to him a few times, and he'd forced sex on her instead. Not that she'd objected at the time.

"There's something else. The strange phone calls I've been getting. I think someone knows you're here with me. And today, when we were swimming, I heard a pod of whales singing and calling to each other. They weren't from my tribe."

"From my tribe?" Roman asked in a burst of excitement.

"I don't know. That's why I came back to shore. If members of your tribe or mine find us together, it will cause problems."

Roman stared at her in disbelief, his brows rising. "Yet you went ahead with our sham marriage?"

"I thought it was for just one date. Enough to slake the lust. I didn't expect to fall in love with you."

Back to the L word again. "I'm going for a swim. We'll discuss this later."

Roman waded into the water, pictured a large orca in his mind, and switched without a hitch. Hot damn. He really was a fish. Elation tore through him, and he slowed for an instant before using his fluke and flippers to speed through the water. It had come back to him. Just as Asia had assured him it would. His memory appeared hazy, but familiar ghosts increasingly stalked his mind.

He was sure it was only a matter of time before his familiar thoughts returned. And as for Asia... Roman blew strongly, a fine mist shooting through his blowhole, before he dived beneath the surface, letting the cool water close over his dorsal fin.

Asia watched him swim away with a mixture of pride and apprehension. Now that he knew the truth, he'd leave. She stood and ambled miserably across the sand. The night had faded, and early dawn lay in waiting. Fatigue made her stumble, and she wiped an angry tear off her cheek. No use crying about what might have been. Roman knew the truth. Their sham marriage would end.

The phone rang as she opened the front door. At this time of the morning, it had to be another of those crank calls. She jerked the phone off the hook. "I have no idea what secret you're talking about, so you needn't call me again."

"Asia? Is anything wrong?" Her mother's well-modulated voice drifted down the line.

Bother. Asia grimaced and rolled her eyes. "Mother. What are you doing ringing me so early in the morning?"

"Just to tell you we've come home early."

"Wasn't the fishing any good in South America?" Shit. Shit. *Shit.* This was not good.

"We didn't make it to South America. Archie ate an octopus. We told him he shouldn't eat the little orange ones, but would he listen? No." A rich chuckle echoed down the line. "Now he's learned the hard way. He won't touch the little blighters again. What are you doing tomorrow? We thought we might come for a visit."

Oh shit. It was worse than she'd imagined. "Ah, sorry, Ma. I'm rehearsing for a new show. How about next week? I should be sorted out by then." Probably an exaggeration. Roman would likely leave the moment he returned from his swim.

"Oh," her mother said. "Oh well. We have domestic chores, and Archie is still throwing up quite a bit. Next week it is then."

Asia hung up with relief. Disaster averted. At least her mother hadn't commented on her greeting or unusual behavior. She must have done a good job of acting normal. Surprisingly, given it felt as if someone had trampled on her heart.

The phone rang again, and Asia scowled. No doubt her aunt this time wanting her to babysit. "Yes?"

"We know your secret," the disembodied voice droned.

"I don't know what you mean." Asia hung up and stared at the phone as if it were an orange octopus. It didn't ring again, and her breath eased out with a relieved sigh.

She strode to the bathroom and flipped on the shower, regulating the temperature to tepid. Asia stepped under the water and wondered what else could go wrong today.

Asia lathered up with peppermint and green apple soap then rinsed the salt off her hair and reached blindly for a bottle of shampoo. The shower door squeaked and her eyes flew open.

"Roman?"

"I've been thinking about us," he murmured in a husky voice.

Asia's heart thudded with apprehension as he joined her in the shower cubicle, closing the door behind him.

"I don't condone lying."

"I don't make a habit of it," Asia said. "It just happened and took on a life of its own."

"Okay." He brushed a kiss over her lips, igniting a flash fire in her body. "Don't lie to me again."

"I won't," Asia promised fervently. Was he giving her a second chance? She was frightened to ask. "Do you remember everything?"

"Just bits and pieces." He kissed her again and nibbled on her bottom lip. "I like you, Asia. I want to see where this might lead, despite the problems we might face."

Asia nodded dumbly, unable to believe her good luck and his generosity.

"So we're agreed? We'll get to know each other with no untruths between us."

Asia smiled. "I'd like that. Very much."

Roman cupped her head with his hands and massaged the shampoo until her hair was clean. He helped her rinse before picking up her soap to lather it over his body. He sluiced off.

"You all done in here?" His gaze drifted downward and lingered on her mouth.

"I want you," Asia murmured.

"You read my mind." Roman shut off the water and shouldered open the shower door. He scooped her off her feet suddenly enough to make her squeak in girly fright.

"The bedclothes will get wet."

"They'll dry." Roman dropped her in the middle of the mattress and followed her down. Asia didn't even bounce before he was over her, kissing her with a fierceness to make her heart pound. Asia caught his urgency and dug her nails into his back. Her legs parted, and moisture seeped from her core.

Roman wanted to make love to her again.

"I'm glad you've remembered some of your past." She angled her neck so he had better access.

"Yeah, my memories are there, just out of reach. At least I was able to shift. That's a start."

"That's great." Asia pressed a kiss to the base of his throat. "My mother rang." Best she tell him the worst now so he couldn't accuse her of keeping secrets. "She wanted to visit, but I put her off."

"Good. We need time together before we deal with our families."

"I had another strange phone call. I think someone knows your identity."

"We'll cope with them too," he promised. "But not right now. I can think of better things to do with our time." Roman delved into her mouth, kissing her deeply, feasting and plundering until pleasure hummed through her veins. Her arms crept up around his neck, and she clutched him tight, reveling in the honesty of the act. He knew the truth, and he was still here. Roman parted her legs and entered her in one long, seamless thrust. His teeth scraped over the frantically beating pulse below her jaw. He felt so long, so thick and hard as he filled her.

"Feels good." Damn, she wished he'd hurry. Slow was all very well, but this time she wanted fast.

"Yeah. Very good." He pulled from her and surged deep again. "I could become addicted to this. To you."

Asia hoped so. She really did. He changed the angle of his strokes, increasing the pace until they were both breathless. *Thank you, God!* He slid a finger across her clit, massaging her lightly. A gasp escaped, the hot fire between her legs almost too much to bear. She writhed and twisted against his body, desperate for release. Hungry little noises escaped her, and he laughed until she contracted her inner muscles.

Roman cursed softly, making her giggle. Then he thrust into her with hard, digging strokes, pushing her over until she shattered, gasping out his name.

"That's it, babe." His large body shuddered as he kept plunging deep, dragging out every last sensation. His ass muscles flexed and he stilled, buried inside her, breathing hard. His eyes glowed when he opened them to stare at her while his heart pounded against her breast. "Thank you. That was amazing."

Asia nodded, the knot in her throat robbing her of speech. She loved this man, and it would kill her if she had to give him up.

They woke an hour later to the shrill ring of the phone.

"Stay there. I'll get it this time." Roman strode from the bedroom toward the kitchen. He snatched it up. "Yes."

Heavy breathing sounded.

"Yes," he repeated with a touch of impatience. He'd

far rather spend time with Asia, repeating the incredible lovemaking. The phone clicked, and he listened to the dead line drone. He replaced the phone with a thump. Possibly a wrong number.

"Who was it? Not someone from my family?" Asia stood in the doorway, dressed in an oversized T-shirt.

"They hung up. Must have been a wrong number."

"Oh. Good." Her shoulders relaxed noticeably.

"Don't worry, babe. What do you want to do for the rest of the day? Have another snooze? Or go swimming again?"

Her face softened, a look of longing making her seem vulnerable. "I'd love to go swimming with you. We could cruise up to Cape Reinga, where the Pacific Ocean meets the Tasman Sea. It's beautiful up there. The color of the ocean..." She trailed off when she saw his expression—one of an intent hunter. "What?"

"You're beautiful." He stepped close and brushed his thumb across her swollen lips. He'd done that and caused the faint love bites on her slender neck. Marks of his possession. He took satisfaction in seeing them, which made him a Neanderthal. This woman filled spaces he hadn't even realized were empty. "And a bit overdressed." He glanced down at his erection, his lips curling to a grin.

"That's okay. Before we go swimming, there's something I want to do." Asia sank to her knees and grasped his thighs to balance. She grinned up at him, and he could see the happiness shine in her face. They had a connection, something new for him because his previous relationships had all been about sex. And pleasure. Never before had he wanted to give unselfishly, expecting nothing in return. This thing with Asia was sex and pleasure wrapped up with joy, happiness, and laughter. He could have added a thousand other things if he were a poet or a writer. Asia had rapidly become his lover and friend.

Laughing, she grasped his cock and set about exploring. She traced his length with her fingers, leaving a path of fire in her wake. Roman forgot their surroundings, the counters and kitchen cabinets fading away, replaced by the magic that was Asia. His cock thickened further under her ministrations.

With a teasing glance at him, she licked across the crown. "I like the way you feel." She did a slow lap over the head and a circle around the slit at the end. "I like the way you taste."

"Is that right?" Roman wondered how far she intended to go with this and if his legs would stand the test.

"Yes," she purred, taking his tip into her hot mouth. With slow laps of her tongue, she teased him, licking away pre-come. Her fingers massaged his tight balls, making him groan.

"God, Asia." His words weren't much more than a harsh groan. His legs trembled and he cupped her head with his hands, all his attention focused on the heat of her mouth, the way she sucked and stroked her tongue across the sensitive underside. Unbidden his hips surged forward, forcing his cock deeper. She never hesitated, her eyes heavy-lidded when she glanced up at him and full of desire. The urge to thrust deeper into her warmth filled him. Her plump, pink lips stretched around his cock seduced him, as did the rhythm of her mouth and tongue—the hot, easy glides that took him deep, teasing his flesh until he shuddered. She kept him balanced on the edge of an explosive climax. He didn't think he'd ever had anyone take such care with him, and it made his heart swell with emotion for her. The curl of her tongue pushed him to the point of no return.

"Asia, I—" Before he could finish, and tell her he needed to pull from her mouth, he came, the intensity of his orgasm blinding and breathtaking. He groaned, his head thrown back as his semen spurted into her mouth. Gradually, his heart rate slowed, and his shaft softened.

Asia released his cock and grinned up at him. "How was that?"

"Damn, Asia." He hauled her to her feet, scooped her up, and placed her on the table. With his hand, he pried her knees apart and moved into the gap he created. "You are amazing." He kissed her lips before feathering kisses down her neck and across her collarbone. He could smell her arousal and wanted to taste that scalding honey. Soon. He kissed and petted her, weighing her heavy breasts in his hands, creating friction between his hands and her T-shirt, exploring until she squirmed. His cock rose again, but he ignored the tension in his groin to concentrate on her pleasure. He whipped the T-shirt over her head and tossed it aside.

Lowering his head again, he licked around the swell of her curves. The scrape of his stubble against the side of one breast made a faint rasping sound. Asia drew a sharp breath when he nipped her, then he soothed the sting with his tongue.

"What are you going to do with me?"

"That's for me to know."

"Will I like it?"

Roman heard the smile in her words. "You might. You might hate it as well." He pushed her back so she rested her weight on her hands and grinned at her before bending over her. He blew a stream of warm air the length of her cleft, noting the glistening folds with pleasure. "I like knowing you want me."

"What's not to want? You make me feel good about

myself." Her head fell back when he applied his tongue. "Oh yes." The words were a ragged whisper.

She made him feel invincible, made him want to please her even more. He ran a finger over her labia, swirling it through her juices and flicking her clit. Teasing and licking, he pushed her toward climax, loving every throaty cry, every sigh he dragged from her. Asia's breathing became deeper, labored, and she trembled. Knowing she was close, he worked harder to make her unravel and lose control. He thrust a single finger into her pussy, pulled back and added another while he flickered his tongue over her swollen nub. Asia gasped, her entire body tensed, and she sobbed out his name while she came.

"Roman."

Smiling his satisfaction, he softened his tormenting strokes until she stopped trembling, allowing her to come back from the high. "You are so responsive. You never hide what you're feeling, and I like that."

"Why would I want to hide how you make me feel?" she asked, sounding astonished.

"Some women do," he said, thinking about Helena, his ex. Now there was a woman who liked getting her way and wasn't above manipulation to swing a situation her way. Frowning, he realized another part of his past had returned and intruded on the present. That's when he knew he swam in deep water. He'd have to hope his family understood and that things wouldn't become as bad as Asia feared. "How about that swim now?"

"Sure."

He lifted her off the table, and they strolled outside, both still naked. They crossed the black sand, still warm from the midday sun, and headed for the water. Waves whooshed to shore, the wind coming in from the sea making them much bigger than earlier. Roman reached for her hand, and his firm grasp brought tears of happiness to her eyes. She skipped a few steps at his side, splashing through the foamy waves as they rushed into shore. They waded into the water until they were waist-deep. Roman tugged her against his chest so their limbs tangled and their lower bodies rubbed together.

"I was sure you'd leave once you learned the truth," Asia said as she relaxed against him. She frowned, enjoying their physical closeness but worried it wouldn't last. Their relationship was so fragile. What if he changed his mind and left?

"Stop." Roman traced a finger over her wrinkled brow. "Let's take that swim to Cape Reinga. Last one there is a rotten egg." He swiftly turned and powered away, leaving Asia staring after him.

The man was so sexy and tempting in either form. He

paused past the point where the waves started to break and spy-hopped to see where she was. Asia waved and, with a grin still on her face, transformed into an orca. Diving through the oncoming wave, she chased after him, the surge of anticipation taking her by surprise. Adrenaline layered with sheer excitement whooshed through her mind.

Swimming with a lover. Wow.

She swam strongly, sounding with a series of clicks and whistles to get a fix on Roman's position. Hopefully, he'd understand her without difficulty.

She had no warning. One moment, he wasn't anywhere nearby, then he swam beneath her, nudging her to the surface. They sprang from the water together, creating a graceful ballet of leaps and huge splashes when they dived back under the water. Roman did a series of twirls before returning to her with a definite smirk.

Show off, she thought, grinning with joy in the knowledge he was better. She sobered quickly. Now if only he would recover his memory.

Roman seemed determined to enjoy the moment and not let her fret. They frolicked like calves, chasing schools of flashing silvery fish, startling and confusing them by blowing bursts of bubbles. The fish crammed together in a tight mass. They were dinner for the taking, but by common consent, they left them and swam farther north.

Asia listened to the static, the garbled speech, and music beneath the sea. No way did she want to run into one of Roman's family members on this little jaunt. But despite her fears, she heard nothing more exciting than a pod of humpback whales heading for Australia and a marital spat between two hammerhead sharks. They took a detour around them. Nothing more unpredictable and plain mean than a pissed shark.

At the tip of the North Island, the ocean met the sea. It was an eerie yet hauntingly beautiful place, the place where the Māori people believe the spirits of the dead depart for their homeland in Waikiki.

Roman nudged Asia, rubbing his snout over the tender skin near her flippers. His touch told her he felt the same magic about the place where the waters met. It was special.

They swam back to Asia's house at a more leisurely pace. Lethargy made Asia's stroking through the water slow and easy. They shifted together in a massive splash of water, their laughter ringing out to add to the music of the beach. Their lips touched in the lazy way of lovers who were familiar with each other.

The killer whale came out of nowhere. Two more came from opposing directions, large black forms with slashes of white attacked, tearing Roman and Asia apart.

Asia screamed, stumbling and going under the water when a wave rushed to shore. She flailed, panic making her forget to breathe. Asia came up gasping for air. Roman had shifted, knowing it was the only way to protect them. Four massive bodies fought, thrashing and sending sheets of water in all directions. Sharp white teeth tore at unprotected flanks while flukes struck lethal blows.

"Ma! Luca!" Asia shouted, recognizing the nicks and scars on her mother and the curly slant of her brother's dorsal fin. Her sister ignored her cries, too, slamming into Roman with enough force to send him flying.

Asia knew she had to do something before Roman was hurt. She threw herself into the melee, screaming at the top of her voice. "Stop it! Leave him alone!"

A fluke caught her in the gut, bleeding the air from her lungs in one thump.

Asia gasped, a wheezy sound, as she struggled to replace the air. Blood dripped from her head, obscuring her vision. She wiped the blood away and saw the fins heading for them.

"Shark. Shark!" she cried. Another fluke caught her across the side of the head, and that was the last thing she recalled before she surrendered to the darkness.

CHAPTER SIX

R oman saw the blow that sent Asia face-first into the water. An incoming wave swept her toward the shore. She didn't move. She didn't come up to breathe. He thrust the attacking whales away with superhuman strength and shifted to human form.

Sharks—where the fuck had they come from—attacked from both sides, thankfully keeping Asia's family busy while Roman attended to Asia. He dragged her up the sand until they were clear of the water.

"Asia, babe." God, she had to be all right. Roman smoothed her hair away from her pale face and tipped back her head. After making sure her airways were clear, he started mouth-to-mouth. Fear stabbed his heart. *Breathe, dammit. Breathe.*

Roman kept going, trying not to think about Asia dying. His family would have done the same thing if they'd caught him kissing Asia. This bloody feud had to stop. It was time for the old ways to change. Past time.

Roman paused midway through the next thought. Hell! He'd remembered. He recalled everything. Their tribes were in a long-running feud. And that wasn't all. Being with him put her in even greater danger than she'd realized. The sharks were probably mercenaries for hire, and Helena's doing.

Asia coughed weakly, her eyelids flickering. Roman held her as she vomited out the seawater she'd swallowed. Thankfully, the bleeding at her temple had slowed. He probed the wound with delicate fingers and decided it didn't need stitches.

Splashing from behind made him glance over his shoulder. Asia's mother, brother, and sister. He watched them shift, his shoulders tensing when they headed toward them with varying expressions on their faces. Roman averted his gaze from their naked bodies. Seeing Asia's mother naked made him uncomfortable.

Asia struggled from his hold. At first, Roman thought she didn't want her family to see her with him, but he realized she wanted to place herself between him and her family in case of problems.

"Get your dirty hands off my sister," a young male shouted, his bronzed face twisted into a scowl.

"Luca." Asia tensed as if she expected her brother to attack again. Her voice was scarcely louder than a whisper.

"If I were Asia, I'd want his hands all over me." The sister fluttered her lashes and cocked one hip to display her assets better.

Roman froze. He didn't like the avid sensuality in her light gray eyes—unusual in an orca. They seemed to pierce straight through him, bringing discomfort and edginess. Damn, he wished he had some clothes.

"Rosa," the last of the trio said, her voice carrying authority. *Lydia Bolino*. He knew her by reputation but hadn't met her in person. She bore a large, strong frame with several scars on her torso. Long black hair spilled down her shoulders, and the strip of white hair at her temple proclaimed her an orca.

After dampening her daughter's enthusiasm, Lydia's attention turned to him and Asia. She frowned when her gaze slid over him. Roman stared back, waiting for her to fire the first salvo. He was determined. No matter what she thought or whatever objections she had, he was not leaving Asia, not unless that was what Asia wanted.

He needed to head back to Auckland Island to sort out the mess he'd left there. Asia could go with him or stay here until he finished, but he intended to keep her indefinitely. They were good together. She made him happy, and he sure as hell hadn't felt that emotion for a long time.

"I hope the two of you have thought this out," she said, surprising Roman with her first words. "Your tribe won't be any happier than us when they learn about the two of you. Do you want to start a war?"

Roman stood and helped Asia to her feet. "We're going to the house to dress and clean up Asia's forehead."

"Fine. We'll be back in an hour to discuss this debacle." Lydia turned and strode into the sea without looking back or checking if Asia's siblings followed.

"You'll be sorry you touched my sister," Luca snarled before he stalked after his mother. He was taller than Asia, although his lack of years meant he didn't have the strength Roman possessed.

"I'm not surprised my sister succumbed to you, big boy." A naughty smile shaped Rosa's lips when she glanced down his naked body. Her gaze drifted back up to his face.

99

"Nice…chest."

"And it's all mine," Asia snapped. "Go find your own stud."

Rosa's dark brows rose. "Well," she said with a slight smirk. She cast another lingering look at Roman before sauntering after her brother and mother. The wench gave an impudent shake of her butt before shifting and diving into the water.

"We'd better attend to that wound," Roman said, amused by her sister despite himself.

"Rosa is a flirt." Asia scowled after her sister. "Pay no attention."

Roman suppressed a grin, instinctively knowing this was not the time to laugh. "I'm not interested in Rosa. Her older sister, now that's another matter."

He pressed his lips to hers. His body reacted immediately, and he chuckled. "See." He gestured at his groin and laughed again. "If we don't hurry, your family will arrive." Roman slid his arm around Asia's waist and directed her to the house. "I'd prefer to meet them with clothes on next time."

"Your memory. It's returned. You didn't seem surprised about anything." Asia halted without warning and turned to him with clear apprehension written across her pale face. "You've remembered everything?"

"Can I come too? I should contact my accompanist about the new bracket of songs we're planning, anyway."

Roman flashed a grin before tracing his fingertips over her parted lips. "I was hoping you'd come with me."

"For sex?" she asked, teasing him now that she felt more secure.

"You betcha." His good humor dispersed. "We can get a special license and get married at the same time." His gaze was intent as he searched her face for a reaction. "What do you think?"

"Yes. Oh yes!" Asia threw her arms around his neck and rained kisses on him, ignoring the protest of sore, aching muscles. Nothing mattered except Roman. "Roman. I love you so much."

"Good." He grinned. "Because I can't imagine life without you."

Roman listened carefully to his younger brother Gene, his gut tightening with each word. "Has Helena openly taken over, or is she just throwing her weight around?"

"She hasn't taken over, but she's considering the move. She's hanging out with shark mercenaries, and that can't be good. You must come home before she turns the

"Yeah, unfortunately. Those phone calls you've been receiving probably relate to a few problems I've been having on the island. The attack on me and the one today too."

A frown appeared on her forehead. "You know who attacked you?"

Roman tugged on her hand, urging her to continue walking. He wanted to soothe her fears and love her all night until dawn. Unfortunately, that wouldn't happen with their families trying to come between them. They hastened up the front path, edged with rustling, native grasses, and Roman pushed open the front door to let her inside. "I have my suspicions. I don't suppose we can drive back to the city so I can collect my gear from the hotel. I have a satellite phone there."

"You can borrow my car if you want. I'm going to bed. I have a headache."

Roman didn't like the dejected set of her shoulders when she turned and headed for the bedroom. He hunted through the bathroom cabinet for first-aid supplies. After pulling out disinfectant, cotton wool, an antiseptic cream, and some headache tablets, he walked to the bedroom to check on Asia.

She lay across the bed, her dark hair fanned across the pillow. Her eyes were closed, and a tiny whistle emerged between parted lips.

Roman hesitated, wondering whether it was safe to leave her sleeping or if he should wake her. She'd certainly seemed lucid enough after she'd come to. While he hesitated, a sharp rap sounded on the front door. Roman grabbed a pair of shorts and pulled them on before going to answer. *A damn short hour*, he thought with a trace of irritation.

He wrenched open the door and stood aside for Asia's family to enter. They arrived en masse, and the open-plan kitchen-dining room was full by the time they'd all entered. Roman bit back a snarl when one of the shifters shoved him out of the way.

"Where's Asia?" her mother demanded.

"She's asleep in the bedroom."

"Kill the bastard," Luca snapped. "He's sleeping with her. I could smell him all over her."

Roman shrugged, unconcerned by the younger male's bluster. "Asia might get upset if you hurt me. She loves me."

Luca sneered, pushing his face close in a threatening manner. "Bah! Feminine crap. She'll get over it."

"That will be enough from you, Luca," Lydia said in a stern voice. It was apparent to Roman that she ruled the family. Her word was final, and they deferred to her in all things. "Healer, please go and check on my daughter. Take Rosa with you."

"Aw, Mother. Can't I stay here?" Here was right beside Roman, standing way too close for his comfort. Her breasts annoyingly rubbed against his arm.

The sisters appeared alike, but Rosa didn't stir his lust. On the other hand, Asia could offer him a tentative smile and turn him inside out.

Lydia Bolino cleared her throat to grab his attention. "What the hell do you think you're doing, Anderson? Your tribe is on the verge of civil war. You should be on Auckland Island, stopping all the petty bickering."

"The workings of my tribe have nothing to do with you." Roman could pull out a leader persona when he needed authority. "Neither is my relationship with Asia."

"Asia is my daughter."

"A mature adult," Roman countered, knowing he wasn't wise to rile the Bolino family when he was the sole Anderson present. Yet he was good at reading other shifters, and although he sensed anger, it was controlled. "An adult ready for marriage."

"Marriage." The word repeated a dozen times until it sounded like an echo bouncing around the house's interior.

"Asia and I intend to cement our relationship with

human legalities."

"And what does Asia say about that? We only have your word." Luca lurched at Roman and swung his fist in a wild punch. Roman felt the breeze when the young male's fist skated past his cheekbone.

"Leave him alone," Asia cried from the bedroom doorway. She looked pale yet beautiful in a royal blue-colored robe. She wobbled, and Roman caught her arm to steady her.

"It's all right. Everything will be fine. Go back to bed and try to sleep. No one will hurt me." Roman guided her into the bedroom, slid her robe off, and tucked her between the cool sheets. The healer stood at the foot of the bed, a scowl on his face, with Rosa at his side, wearing a mischievous grin. With a reassuring smile at Asia, he left to face her family again.

"I want to talk to Asia." Asia's mother walked past Roman into the bedroom and closed the wooden door with a sharp snap.

She was back minutes later with the healer and Rosa and made a sharp gesture with her hand. The family members filed from the house with low muttering and threats.

"Don't think you've won this battle, Anderson," she snarled. "You might have won this round, but my daughter will come to her senses." She stomped to the doorway then turned to glare at him, a tall, imposing woman with glossy black hair and a distinctive white lock at her temple. "You will marry Asia over my dead body."

When Asia woke the next morning, the house was still and quiet. No arguments. That could be a good thing, or it could mean there were dead bodies littering her lounge. Had Roman left? The thought brought a frown and niggling uncertainty. He wasn't worth the stress if he'd left because of her family. She'd get over him. One day soon.

Asia forced away thoughts of Roman and things she couldn't control. A gingerly stretch caused a wince of protest from sore muscles. Either her brother or sister had landed some good blows. Her ribs ached something fierce. When she glanced down at her arm, she noticed the deep purple bruise. She grimaced. No wonder she was feeling sore.

She grabbed her robe, padded down the passage, and peeked through the doorway into the lounge. No blood or bodies. After checking the rest of the house, she discovered it was empty. A folded blanket draped across the couch in the lounge told her Roman had spent the night. At least she hoped it was Roman and not one of her family members. She headed to the bathroom and flicked on the water.

Hopefully, the warm water would relieve some of the stiffness in her body.

Twenty minutes later, she entered the kitchen and plugged in the kettle. The sound of the front door opening and closing made her whirl. Her heart jumped like a racehorse leaping from a starting gate. Her hand slid across the kitchen counter to curl around the handle of a carving knife. "Who's there?"

"Asia? What are you doing out of bed so early?" Roman strode into the kitchen, bringing the tang of the sea and outdoors. His dark gaze traveled lazily up and down her body. There was a sexual intensity to his gaze, but concern as well. "You feeling okay?"

"A bit sore. I'll live. I thought you'd left." Asia quashed her blaze of nerves and forced a smile as she released the carving knife. She pulled two mugs from the cupboard. "Is Mother right about a possible war?"

"There was unrest when I left, and according to rumors your mother has heard, things have worsened. I need to finish the business discussions I came to Auckland for before I return to the island." Roman sauntered up to her to brush a kiss across her lips.

Asia shuddered at the intense, searing emotion that shot through her at his touch. The phone rang and fear ratcheted up the tension inside her. More weird calls?

"I'll get it." Roman plucked up the phone. "Yeah? Who is this?" The phone crashed back down. "Heavy breather."

Asia swallowed to settle her jumping nerves. "I wish they'd quit calling. If they want to freak me out they're succeeding."

"Try not to worry, babe. It's me they're trying to harass."

That made sense, except... "Maybe, but how did they get this number? Oh, never mind. I'm listed. It wouldn't be difficult. I want to ask you something else. Did you mean it? About marrying me?" She tried to keep the neediness and uncertainty from her voice and failed dismally. Dammit, she needed reassurance if she was going to rebel against unwritten family law.

Roman cupped her face with his hands. "I meant every word. The feud between our tribes is ridiculous. If you ask the elders, I'm sure they won't remember the feud's origin. Besides, the woman I love is part of the Transients. I didn't plan for it to happen, but it has." His stern mouth softened into a smile that made hope bloom inside Asia. Rosa had been wrong and so had her mother. He wasn't after a scalp to attach to his dorsal. This was love. "It's past time to end the feud. I still need to go back to the city."

island into a military state. Gads, you should see the way her cronies strut about the town with barely concealed weapons."

"There's been a problem with brokering the treasure. I've had to set up new meetings for next week."

"Damn," Gene muttered. "The end of next week might be too late."

Roman hesitated, wondering if anyone might be trying to listen in on their call. The hair at the back of his neck prickled as it had before the attack, yet he hadn't been able to catch out his watchers. "I'd hoped to take a holiday before I head back to the island."

"A holiday?" his brother yelped. "Time for that later. You're needed here."

"I can't come back right now." Roman cut through his brother's bluster. "Besides, I want to bring someone with me."

"A woman?" His brother sounded shocked. "Man. Helena is going to be pissed. Who? Do I know her?"

"I don't think so. We'll discuss it when I get back to the island." Too bad about Helena's feelings. She'd have to deal with this final rejection. Roman was aware Helena still thought of him as her property. Her maneuvering to stop other women getting close amused him. Most of the time. The female orca wanted power. Oh, she'd coated it up with sweet smiles and sex, and it had taken him time to see through her manipulation. Discovering her in bed with another orca during the summer games had torn away his blinders. Roman refused to share. After telling her their relationship was over, he'd walked away. It appeared Helena hadn't accepted his edict.

Roman scowled. The rumors from Asia's mother and his brother's demands for him to return home brought conflict. The tribe needed him, but he wanted to do something for himself for the first time in his life instead of putting the tribe first. "It's none of Helena's business who I see."

Roman heard raised voices on his brother's end.

"Wait a sec," his brother said.

Roman was unable to decipher words, but the tone was unmistakable. Panicked.

"Bro, Helena and two of her brothers have disappeared. They seem to have left the island, but the rest of the gang is here. Roman, I don't like this. Helena's people openly wear weapons and order residents to stay indoors."

Roman cursed, low and pithy. "Damn, Gene. I have to make at least the first meeting. They're calling me back to confirm a time, but missing the last meeting has made negotiations tense. They don't trust me to deliver."

"Do you think Helena had something to do with the

attack? Maybe slowing up negotiations on purpose?" Gene asked.

"A good possibility." Roman had wondered the same thing. His gut churned while he debated his course of action. "I didn't see faces, but there were three of them. Has Helena left the island before?"

Gene hesitated. "I was away for a few days on general patrol. I'll ask around."

"Thanks." Roman dragged a hand through his hair and wished he had more time. "I'll check back with you in a few hours once I know what's going on this end."

Roman walked to the business meeting since it was to take place at the Imperial Hotel, a five-minute stroll on a fine day. When he left the Odyssey Inn where he was staying, his senses told him he was under surveillance. Damn if he could see who was watching. A casual glance over his shoulder when he crossed the street didn't catch his watchers out. Roman paused at the next set of traffic lights, waiting for the signal for pedestrians to cross. The traffic halted, and Roman started across.

A battered blue sedan failed to stop and continued across the intersection, the wheels spinning when the driver floored the accelerator. Roman froze for an instant. The driver was trying to hit him! He threw himself out of the path of the oncoming vehicle, hitting the ground with a painful thump before rolling to safety. The car continued past.

"Man, he tried to hit you!" A young male dumped the backpack he'd had draped off one shoulder on the ground and helped Roman to stand.

"Are you all right, young man? Should I call the police?" an elderly woman asked.

Roman thought for a moment that she intended to check for broken bones. He dusted off his suit. It had all happened so fast he hadn't seen the driver, but one thing was clear. That was no accident. The driver had intended to run him down.

"Thanks. I'm fine." Roman limped down the street to make his appointment.

The meeting went well, better than he'd expected. Gerald Jones was willing to buy the items they'd found in the sunken ship, or family heirlooms, as he'd told Gerald Jones and his team. They didn't want anyone poking around near their island, searching for sunken treasure. Roman cursed the day they'd found the ship. Greed had ripped the tribe apart, with Helena and her followers wanting to keep the treasure for a select few. Roman had decided to use the proceeds to make improvements on the island. The debate continued, but the fighting had turned mean and dirty.

Roman took the elevator to his hotel room. When he arrived outside, the door was propped open. He walked inside, expecting to find the maids cleaning. Instead, he discovered his clothes, paperwork, and toiletries littering the floor.

"Asia? Asia! Are you here?" Hell, if they'd hurt Asia, he'd never forgive himself. He grabbed the phone and rang Asia's cell phone number. His panic eased when she answered. Low music, a piano, and the wail of a saxophone were audible down the line.

"Hey, Asia. You almost finished there? Ready to get hitched?"

"I'll meet you at the courthouse in half an hour." The excitement in her voice brought a smile, albeit brief. He hoped he wasn't putting Asia in danger by marrying her. They could always postpone the ceremony until another time. No, dammit! He wanted Asia by his side. He wanted to sleep with her and wake up with her in the morning.

"Half an hour," he confirmed. "Don't be late."

"It's fashionable for the bride to arrive late," she teased.

"After my morning, I don't think my heart could take it. I think I'll put you over my knee if you're late."

"Ooh! Be still, my heart," she cooed. "Is something wrong?"

Roman laughed, seeking to reassure her. He didn't want her to change her mind either. "Nothing I can't handle."

Asia checked her watch. The bride was supposed to arrive late, not the groom.

"Yes, well. I'm sorry, dear." The marriage registrar pushed his frameless spectacles up his nose. "I have ceremonies arranged for the rest of the afternoon. You'll have to reschedule."

Asia gritted her teeth and tried to hold the tears at bay. He'd changed his mind about marrying the enemy. Her family had tried to tell her.

Stop it. Wait to hear his explanations before jumping to conclusions.

"Thank you. We'll reschedule." She forced a smile on seeing the sympathetic expression on the elderly gentleman's face. He thought Roman had changed his mind. The marriage registrar felt sorry for her.

She had to get out of here before she did something stupid like cry. Asia hurried from the courthouse into the sunshine outside. She made it halfway across the square outside before the first tear ran down her cheek.

She waited at home by the phone for the rest of the afternoon, her mood swinging from tearful to furious and back again.

Roman didn't come. He didn't call.

CHAPTER SEVEN

"F or the last time, Helena and her brothers have taken over the island! Don't you care?"

Roman stared at his brother before averting his gaze and looking at the landscape below. They flew over an open expanse of ocean, heading due south to Auckland Island. Asia would think the worst, and he had no way to contact her.

"Of course I care," he snapped. Maybe if he took care of

this mess, he could fix things with Asia. If she'd talk to him. "I thought they'd disappeared."

"They're back. She's wearing a flashy ring and telling people you're getting married, that she's acting on your behalf. Any of your friends who deny her story have disappeared. I don't know whether they're dead or are incarcerated somewhere. People fear her because she's shown she's not afraid to kill those who oppose her will. You should have been here to stop her. You shouldn't have left and given her the opening to seize control."

"I was the only one who could negotiate the treasure sale without giving away the wreck's location. I would have been here if I could." Roman didn't see why he needed to explain himself to Gene. Surely his brother knew he had the interests of the tribe at heart.

The two brothers glared at each other, the taut silence full of resentment and irritation on Roman's part.

The helicopter landed on the island's far side, away from the village and prying eyes. They waited for Tom, the pilot, to secure the aircraft and join them for the drive into town.

"Tom, let us out on the outskirts of town so I can show Roman how bad things are here," his brother instructed.

"You're being paranoid, practically kidnapping me and sneaking me back onto the island." Frustration simmered through Roman. Asia would hate him. Hell, he'd be on her family's hit list for leaving and breaking her heart.

"Well, I don't understand what was so important that you couldn't return," his brother muttered.

"I was getting married, dammit!"

Both Gene and Tom turned to gape at Roman. The vehicle veered toward the edge of the cliff.

"Watch the road," Roman barked.

"I thought you were just sleeping with the woman, stringing her along." His brother sounded accusing. "You never indicated it was serious. You haven't been away for long. Who is it? Not a human? That will go down well."

Tom glanced at him, full of nosy interest, before concentrating on the winding road that cut along the edge of a cliff. Roman could practically see his ears flapping.

The truth had to come out eventually. "Asia Bolino." Roman waited for the fallout.

"Asia? I don't believe the name is..." His brother's mouth dropped open, and his eyes bulged so much he resembled a fish. "Bolino? Fuck! Roman, have you lost your mind?"

The vehicle went precariously close to running off the road.

"Perhaps you should pull over," Roman said. "Then you can both have your say about the state of my mind."

Tom stopped the vehicle. "Bolino? As in a member of

the Transients?"

Roman gave a curt nod.

"The enemy," the pilot muttered. "That's all we need to add to this little war we've got going down here."

Roman thought his brother had exaggerated. It was worse. Helena's people patrolled the town armed with weapons. Shark mercenaries and Helena's orca supporters stood on most corners, and they had to take a circuitous route through the town to avoid a confrontation. It seemed they'd put a curfew in place, and the central part appeared quiet and empty. The lamps that lit the square near the council building weren't burning, either shot out or switched off. The atmosphere was one of fear, and the few orcas he saw darted out of sight on glimpsing them. Gene was right. The distrust on their faces told Roman they believed he and Helena were one and the same.

His brother put a hand on his shoulder, offering silent support. "Helena has taken over the council chambers. It would be best if you went to your cottage. I will pass the word to those loyal to you."

Roman took exception to his brother's orders. "I'd rather confront Helena now."

"Wait until the morning. See how many orcas are still loyal to you," Gene said gruffly.

Roman gave a curt nod, seeing the wisdom of the suggestion. When he arrived at his cottage, it felt as if he'd been away for years. He prowled the interior, worrying about Asia. For the first time in his memory, the fate of his people was secondary to his personal life. Somehow, he had to return to Asia to reassure her of his love. The night passed slowly while he debated alternatives and the quickest way to return to Asia.

The next morning, Roman spent an hour listening to complaints about Helena and her brothers, his anger steadily building with each new revelation. The trio had done their job well, sowing the seeds of mistrust and shifting loyalty from Roman to their cause. But there were still orcas on the island who thought as he did. To survive and prosper, they needed to put money back into the island's infrastructure.

The treasure wasn't going anywhere while Helena held the village at gunpoint. But they needed to keep to the terms of the contract he'd arranged while on the mainland. The village needed the money for improvements, for a better life for all the inhabitants. How did he start to repair the cracks that had appeared in his tribe? No doubt, becoming involved with Asia would make things worse.

He dragged his hand through his hair and leaned back in the wooden chair. It creaked in protest. Tendrils of pain curled through his temples in the start of a headache. Fresh air, he decided. The legs of the chair thumped onto the tiled floor, and he stood abruptly.

Five minutes later, he strode from his cottage, openly defying Helena and her brothers. If they wanted a confrontation, they could have one. Thoughts of the female orca brought a scowl. She was a loose cannon. *A kook*.

Roman stomped down the cobblestone road and turned left to the beach. He kicked off his leather sandals and left them where they landed. The sand was cool beneath his feet. A strong wind blew, ruffling his hair and sending the waves crashing into shore. A snort escaped. Fit his mood perfectly. He checked his watch and thought about Asia. Picturing her in his mind soothed the rough edges of his irritation.

Asia was the one good thing to come from this entire mess. He hoped she would forgive him for leaving without a word. Roman ceased his stomping and slowed to an amble. A seal barked, setting off the nesting seabirds on the nearby cliff.

Roman caught a flash of color in his peripheral vision. A gun fired. The seals barked again in agitation, shooting off the rocks into the safety of the water while the seabirds took off in a mass of squawks and a flurry of white feathers. Another shot sounded.

Closer. Then a third grazed his cheek. Roman leapt for cover behind a rock formation, his pulse racing. Hell. Where were they? He couldn't see anyone. His hand went up to his face and came away with a trace of blood. Cautiously, he explored the wound. Not too bad, but it stung like the devil. He dabbed at it with his shirt before peering around the rock. He still couldn't see anything, but the seabirds had settled again, which indicated the intruders had departed.

Roman waited a little longer and ventured from cover, ready to leap back behind the rock at the first sign of danger. Nothing happened. But he didn't intend to make himself an easy target. He darted from rock to rock, heading for the copse of gnarled trees not far from the beach. Once there, he scurried from rocks to dried grass-like toitoi bushes until he reached the village. It seemed Helena had relaxed her rule. Several orcas went about their daily business in the main thoroughfare, and Roman decided it was safe to move openly with everything looking so normal.

"Ah, Roman." The feminine voice was low and gloating. "You've decided to show your face."

Roman turned to face Helena. The orca was stunning, very beautiful with long, flowing dark hair. A thin plait emphasized the strand of white at her temple while she'd poured her curvy body into a tight black polo jersey and black jeans. A pair of black boots completed the outfit. The woman was confident. Arrogant. Greedy. If she had her way, the treasure would go into her pockets. The orca had an insatiable thirst for material possessions, as evidenced by the ostentatious ring on her left hand.

"Helena. I thought you'd left the island."

"Had an accident?" she cooed, ignoring his comment. "Darling, you're so clumsy."

Two could play that game. Roman shrugged. "Nothing life-threatening."

Helena's two brothers moved up to flank her. They presented a united front with almost identical expressions of amusement.

"Tell us the location of the treasure," she demanded.

"So you can loot the wreck." Roman shook his head. "I don't think so."

"It's possible you might change your mind," Helena cooed again.

Roman didn't like her reaction. Too controlled, and not a hint of her usual fiery temper. "I don't think so." If orcas believed they intended to marry, she'd planted her poison well.

"Not even if you learned we have your girlfriend?" one of Helena's brothers asked.

Asia? But how did they know? Wait. If they were responsible for the phone calls and attacks in the mainland, they would know about Asia. He stared, keeping his face impassive to conceal his panic. They'd need to keep quiet about Asia's importance to him because the islanders would learn they'd been lying about him and Helena. A possible way to wrest back control.

Gene stepped from the nearby building to stand beside Helena and her brothers. Shock roared through Roman. *His own brother. Hell, he hadn't seen that coming.*

"You should never have become involved with a Transient, Roman," Gene snarled. "You're a traitor."

Roman stared through the bars covering the grubby window, his fear for Asia making his stomach roil. He didn't care what they did to him, but he couldn't bear the thought of Asia dragged into the middle of his fight with Helena. They were lying. They had to be. Asia's family wouldn't allow them to harm her. He paced to the door, and even though he knew it was locked, he attempted to open it again.

Sparse light entered through the small window, enough for him to see from one side of the room to the other and know it was secure. A generator hummed in the distance. Roman stalked the perimeter, searching for a way to escape imprisonment. Finally, he dropped to the concrete floor and sat with his back pressed against the damp wall, trying to subdue his fear. Like an insidious beast, it writhed inside him until he tasted it. Smelled it. Felt the rapier-sharp claws.

He had to face the truth—he was stuck here to await Helena's decree regarding his fate. And there was nothing he could do to help Asia.

Roman jumped to his feet. Dammit, he refused to give up. There had to be something he could do. Think! He glanced up and froze, his eyes widening. A hole to access the roof. A slow smile crossed his lips while he debated the best way to approach his escape attempt.

The grate of a key in the lock pulled him from his contemplation. Roman sauntered closer to the door, every inch of him alert. Perhaps an easier way? He tensed, ready to grab any opportunity.

The door creaked when it opened. A male with a thickset body slid through the gap and glanced over his shoulder before partially closing the door. Roman recognized the helicopter pilot.

Tom handed Roman a plate. Raw fish. Despite hunger pangs, Roman ignored the food. "What's happening?"

"They've summoned everyone in the village to a meeting. Hurry, we don't have much time. We have to get you out. You're the only one who can stop this madness. They're expecting me back as soon as I deliver the food."

"They'll know you let me out."

Tom paused for an instant. "That can't be helped. There's no other alternative. We have to get you off the island."

Roman sorted through the scenarios available to him. He could swim, but that would take at least two days, and he couldn't take much in the way of luggage. Damn, he needed to make the delivery to take the heat from Helena's argument. Without the treasure, there was less leverage. Obviously, Helena hadn't discovered he'd shifted the booty to a new location. Two others knew, and Roman hoped they were safe and still held the same views as he. They needed the proceeds for the good of the tribe. "I don't suppose you would fly me to the mainland?"

The pilot's dark eyes twinkled with excitement. "An adventure," he said. "Hell, yeah. I thought you'd never ask!"

"If Helena learns of your part in my escape, she'll make

your life difficult," Roman warned.

Tom snorted with contempt. "She's a greedy bitch who gets off on power. If we let her, she'll ruin our island paradise."

"Good. Here's what we'll do to buy some time. See the access hole up there? Hoist me up, and I'll escape through there. Then leave and lock the room. Go back to the meeting and pretend everything is all right. I'll meet you over on the other side of the island by the helicopter."

Tom wasted no time in carrying out Roman's suggestion. Roman pushed the access cover out of position and squeezed through. He signaled to Tom before sliding the cover back, but leaving it a fraction off center. Hopefully, that would leave the pilot free of suspicion. It would be a difficult feat to get up to the access hole on his own, but not impossible for someone of his body strength. Making his way quietly through the crawl space between the roof and the ceiling, he slid the next exit hole he came across aside.

A body moved in the far corner of the room. "Who's there?" a deep voice rumbled.

Elation poured through Roman. He recognized the voice. Victor, one of his friends. "Roman. Care to break this joint?"

Within seconds, Victor knelt beside him. "Good to see

you, mate."

"Anyone else in here we should liberate?"

"Yeah, Weed and Smith are here somewhere. Helena and her kooky brothers locked us up last week when we started to ask too many questions."

"Ah." Roman's grin held pure wickedness. "Just the orcas I need to kick some ass."

"I told you the Resident Orca was a lowdown pile of useless shit," Luca snarled. "Good riddance, I say."

Asia bit back a retort, knowing that was what Luca wanted. More of the same. As if she didn't feel low enough already. Roman had walked away without a word. Intelligence from the rest of the tribe had informed her of his return to Auckland Island. Asia believed them despite the hurt engendered by his abandonment. They had no reason to lie.

"Aren't you going to say anything?" Luca prodded.

"Piss off. Leave me alone." Asia turned her back on her brother and walked into the apartment bedroom. Grabbing a bag, she tossed underwear inside before yanking open the wardrobe.

"What are you doing?" Luca demanded.

"Packing."

"You're not going to him?"

Asia fumbled the bottle of shampoo and conditioner she'd retrieved from the bathroom. Heaven help her, but she wanted to go to Roman, even if it was to punch him in the nose for hurting her so much. "I'm going to the beach for the weekend. I'm tired after rehearsals this week."

"I'm going with you."

Not if she had anything to do with it. Asia threw a toilet bag inside her larger bag and zipped it closed. "I'll drop you off at home before I leave."

"I'll ring mother," he warned.

She stared at him in disbelief. "You're gonna tell on me like you did when we were young?"

"I'm worried about you. We all are."

Asia picked up her bag and left the apartment with Luca dogging her heels. Maybe she should have company at the house. His presence would stop her brooding.

"I've changed my mind. You can come with me, but don't mention Roman or we'll have an argument and I'll toss you out."

Luca gave a curt nod. "I'll drive."

"Fine."

As Asia suspected, the house was full of memories. She took one look at the bed where they'd made love and decided to sleep in the spare room. "You sleep in here." She averted her gaze and closed her mind to the memories of Roman's mouth on hers, how it felt to join intimately with him. The way he made her think she could fly. Asia blinked away the memories. She needed a glass of wine. Too bad if it made her giggly. She could do with a good laugh. Luca had forced his company on her. He could deal with the consequences.

CHAPTER EIGHT

"**I**'m going for a swim to clear my head," Asia said. A man with a hammer pounded away inside her brain, making her regret the amount of wine she'd consumed the night before.

"I don't think you should swim alone."

"Don't push." Asia jumped to her feet and immediately grabbed her skull with both hands. The bloody little man had gone berserk with his thumping. He had drummer aspirations.

"How long will you be?"

"As long as it takes." Asia left the house without looking back, stomping over black sand already warm beneath her bare feet. She winced at the bright sunlight, squinting in the hope of filtering out the worst of the glare. She was never gonna drink again.

At the high tide mark, she shed her clothes and left them where they fell. She meandered to the water so she didn't disturb the man with the hammer. The waves rushed to shore and receded. Asia breathed deeply in an effort to settle her churning tummy. The salty tang of the sea didn't help with her ailment. She waded through the water until waist deep, then shifted and dived through the next wave that rushed to shore. The aches and pains faded as Asia swam lazily out to open water.

Roman drove like a madman to Asia's house on the beach. He'd hoped they'd find Asia at the apartment or the club. No such luck. The closer they got to Asia's house, the deeper Roman's concern. Instinct told him Asia was in extreme danger, while frustration simmered through him because of the problems they'd had getting here. Three wasted days while they found a way to leave the island because someone had vandalized the chopper. Helena had disappeared again and was probably here, trying to block the sale of the treasure.

He hadn't seen his brother since he'd crossed lines to join the enemy. He still couldn't believe Gene had sold him out and placed Asia in danger.

Victor leaned over from the backseat. "Careful, mate. We want to arrive in one piece."

Roman slowed before forcing the accelerator closer to the floor. It wasn't Victor's fiancée in danger. The sedan's wheels shrieked when he drove through an S-bend. The speedometer flickered upward as Roman pushed the car to its limits. He pulled up outside Asia's house with a screech of brakes. The driver's door flew open and Roman sprinted from the car, leaving the engine running. He wrenched open the front door and raced inside Asia's house.

"Asia!" Roman hurried from room to room. He checked the bedroom, hoping she'd be there—safe. Someone stirred in the bed. Hope surged and died. It wasn't Asia. "Luca, where's Asia?"

Luca leapt from the bed and grabbed him by the throat so quickly that Roman didn't have time to protect himself. He slammed up against the wall with Luca tightening his grip on Roman's throat. "Bastard. Leave my sister alone."

"Need some help there, Roman? The others are still in the car. You want me to get them?"

Luca tensed on hearing Victor's voice.

"We're not here to cause trouble," Roman said. "Where's Asia?"

Luca scowled. "Out swimming."

"Alone? Shit! Listen, she's in danger. Helena is after her. She knows I love Asia."

"Chicken shit, you left her standing at the courthouse. You walked out on her without a word. That's not love."

"I love her," Roman gritted out. Hell they didn't have time for this crap. Asia was out swimming alone. "Call your family, all the members of your tribe. Please, she's in danger. We need to work together. Both tribes."

"Well, there's a concept," a feminine voice drawled from the doorway. "Luca, I'm glad you rang and suggested I talk to Asia in person," Lydia Bolino drawled. "I wouldn't miss this for the world."

Roman, Victor, and Luca turned to face the matriarch of the Bolino tribe. Roman explained the situation and his fears.

Asia's mother listened and made a quick decision. "Luca, call the tribe. Now." Her son glared at Roman and Victor before he stomped from the bedroom. Asia's mother ignored her son's ill temper. "I assume the members of your tribe will agree to a cessation of hostilities while we search for Asia."

"You have my word," Roman said. Urgency held him in its grip. Asia was in danger. He needed to find her, to hold her, to ensure she was safe from Helena and the other rebels.

"Excellent. Let us go." Asia's mother strode down the beach with Roman and Victor following. She calmly stripped and marched into the ocean, shifting as soon as the water was deep enough.

Roman gestured for the other two to join them.

"Well, mate," Victor drawled, still staring after the orca cutting through the water. "I can see what the fuss is about, if your lady's ass is as fine as her mother's."

"You're sick." Weed shook his head in a disparaging manner.

"I can't help it if I have a thing for older women." A small smile played on Victor's lips. "Don't knock experience until you try it."

"Enough." Roman cut through the crap. He glanced down the beach and saw others shifting and diving through the incoming waves. "The Bolinos have arrived. I've given my word we will hold the peace. No attacks or violence toward the Bolinos. Save it for Helena and the rebels."

They tore off their clothes and dropped them on the sand. Roman sprinted into the water and shifted seamlessly. He sucked in a breath and dived beneath the water, casting out a series of soft vocal clicks. Victor, Weed, and Tom swam nearby.

They answered and fanned out to cover a wider area. On his right, another series of clicks indicated that Asia's family and tribe were calling for her. Luckily, the language was similar enough for them to get the gist and maintain close communication.

They'd find Asia before Helena captured her. There was no other alternative.

Asia swam aimlessly without a specific destination in mind. She allowed the cool water to soothe her aching head and only surfaced when necessary. The angle of the seabed deepened, and seaweed waved gently with the current. Schools of fish darted in and out of the rock formations, shying from her in case she was hunting. Asia ignored them but found it difficult to disregard the loneliness that swept over her without warning. Roman had crept into her heart, and his leaving had left a gaping hole that continued to bleed. She didn't understand what had happened to make him run. She'd tried to contact him via satellite phone, but he didn't answer any calls. Screening his callers, no doubt.

A gray shape swam in front of her before disappearing behind rocks. Asia hesitated but relaxed when it didn't reappear, continuing on her meandering journey through the valley created by the huge boulders and the water's currents.

Harsh clicks of an unfamiliar dialect cut through the peace of the undersea world. Asia stopped, her heart pounding with apprehension. A great white shark swam in front of her, and she relaxed. One shark, she could cope with without difficulty.

She flicked her fluke to propel herself through the water and headed for the shark. The last thing she wanted was to show fear. When she was halfway through the valley, several orcas appeared in front of her. Guttural clicks bounced off the rocks as they communicated. The strange dialect. Asia understood two words in every four or five, but one thing was clear.

Danger.

Asia turned, intending to exit the same way she'd entered. Three sharks and an orca waited for her, blocking her path to freedom.

Up. The sole way out of this mess was up.

Asia swam strongly, leaping from the water.

Surrounded.

Fear bloomed along with confusion. Why were they targeting her? Who were they? She splashed back into the water and gave a distress call. Please let someone from her clan hear. *Please be there, Luca.*

One of the orcas approached Asia, its mouth open in a smirk. Asia backed up.

She repeated her distress call, and the orca's grin widened. Asia refused to do nothing. Big for her sex, she might make it if she rushed them. Take them by surprise.

Decision made, Asia acted. She propelled her body through the water, heading away from the female and straight for the sharks and orcas at the other end of the valley.

At the last moment, she realized they'd strung a net over the exit. *Too fast.* She was going too fast. Asia crashed into the net. The force of her impact sent the sharks and two orcas backward. For a second, she thought she'd make it, but their combined strength held. The net wrapped around her body and held her prisoner under the water.

Air. She needed to breathe. They intended to keep her underwater, murdering her. If anyone found her body, the presence of the net would place the blame on humans.

Everyone would assume her death was an accident. Icy fear hit then. Her family. She'd never see them again. She would never see Roman again. Never be able to tell him she loved him. Never have the opportunity to smack him one for acting the bastard.

She was going to die.

But she didn't intend to go without a fight. Asia whacked a shark in the face with her fluke. Furious, the creature slashed with its teeth, drawing blood. The other sharks attacked, biting and hacking through the net and flesh with their lethal teeth. Pain lashed her. She struggled violently, fighting and muscling her way to the surface. The harder she fought, the more tangled the net became, wrapping around her body, holding her fast. Lack of air made her mind hazy. Black dots appeared before her eyes. She cried out, the clicks of distress lost in frenzied calls of the strangers.

Roman paused and sent out a series of clicks. "Did you hear that?" he called to the others when they closed up their fanned search line. "That sounded like Helena. Weed, go and summon one of the Bolinos. Tell them they're in the canyon, if you can get them to understand."

He raced off in the direction of the excited chatter, swimming faster than he'd ever swum before. Panic wrapped around him, clinging and threatening to swallow him alive. Asia. What if Helena killed her? Hell, that was a given. She'd want to show strength. Killing a Bolino would show her followers she was serious and wouldn't quibble about annihilating the other clan—their enemies.

Asia would die thinking he'd deserted her.

The sharks saw them first. They hesitated, and Roman and his clan members attacked. The water churned white. Flukes inflicted lethal blows. Teeth slashed at unguarded flanks. Blood seeped into the water.

"The Bolinos are here," Victor called. "Find Asia."

Roman needed no urging. Fear for Asia propelled him to speed. Fury at Helena. He'd find the traitorous bitch and force her to give answers.

He heard a familiar voice issuing orders. Helena. The orders sent a chill surging through the length of his body. Asia. They had her.

"*Drown the bitch*," Helena snarled. "Make it look like an accident."

A net. Guarded. Damn, he needed backup. He turned to see who was available, and to his great relief, he saw Luca and his mother fast approaching. He didn't hesitate. He swam directly at the net from below. Asia needed air.

He prayed she was conscious enough to breathe on her own. Roman shunted Asia upward, casually flicking off two sharks that dared to take issue. An orca charged, but Roman ignored it, putting his faith in the Bolino clan. Blood seeped from wounds along her body. Shit, it was fortunate the sharks hadn't gone into a feeding frenzy. Obviously, they feared Helena more. The worst gash was at her throat, and the net they'd captured her in clung to her body. It was strong, made from some sort of nylon. He'd need a knife. Roman held her weight above the surface of the water until the need to breathe made him seek the air. To his relief, he detected an erratic pulse. She lived.

For the moment.

A dark shape darted toward him. *Helena*. Roman steeled himself for the blow, but it didn't come. Weed and Victor seized Helena, driving her off, and Roman concentrated on Asia.

Gradually, the waters around them stilled. Roman glanced around and saw orcas from the Bolino clan and his friends had surrounded them in a protective circle.

Asia's mother advanced with an older orca, its dorsal fin skewed to the side. They both nudged Asia. Communication took place, a series of low-pitched squeaks and singing. Roman found he understood most of their chatter. He vocalized in return.

"Back to shore," Asia's mother said.

The journey back to the beach near Asia's house took longer than Roman expected. The net snagged on rocks and trapped Victor. Asia's mother organized a rescue while Roman kept Asia afloat.

"Hurry," he urged, hearing the trace of panic in his vocals. A shiver racked Asia. *Shock*. Damn, they had to hurry.

Two of the orcas yanked on the net. Victor swam free, and Roman noticed him nuzzling Asia's mother before they swam on. Roman snorted with a quick flash of amusement. Victor never lost an opportunity to score, and the age difference wasn't significant in orca terms.

Finally, they reached the shore. Roman held Asia above water while the others shifted. When they had her, he moved away and shifted.

"A knife," he hollered. "Someone get a knife to cut her free. Where are the healers?" He took in her still form, his fear escalating. "Will she be able to change?"

"I don't know." Her mother's dark hair lay plastered against her head, contrasting sharply with the paleness of her cheeks. She shivered, and Victor appeared at her side, his usual grin absent.

He slipped an arm around her waist. "The healer is here.

He will know."

A Bolino handed Roman a knife, and they hacked the net from her still body. Roman held her, making sure she didn't drown yet keeping her skin moist.

The healer ran gnarled hands over her wounds. "Most are superficial," he muttered.

Roman glanced at her head. "Apart from this one at her throat, and the one on her chest. They look the worst."

Asia moaned and winced when the healer probed the wound. Her blowhole contracted.

Relief swept through Roman. Tears stung his eyes, but he ignored them.

"She's coming to." His voice emerged rich with emotion—everything he felt for Asia all rolled up in those three words. "Asia, can you hear me?"

"She's trying to shift," the healer murmured.

The air shimmered around her. Roman saw her pale features flash in an out.

"Come on, babe. You can do it."

Then the shimmering ceased, and she appeared in her human form. Asia collapsed, unable to stand on her own. A wave washed over her head before Roman could seize her. She coughed weakly as he carried her up the beach. The gurgling sound didn't sound reassuring. The gaping wound at her throat brought fury. Helena would pay for this atrocity.

A sharp blast—a series of whistles—filled the silence.

"Intruder alert," one of the Bolinos said tersely. "We set a guard at the entrance. It's private but we didn't want any surprises today."

"Everyone dress before they think this is a nudist colony," Victor quipped.

There was a mad scramble for clothes.

"I'll get yours," Victor said to Roman and Asia's mother. "Go."

Roman scooped Asia up and ran for the house. Once inside, he placed her on the bed. It was bad. He didn't need a healer to tell him that.

"Leave. Summon Marge," the healer added. "I'll need another to help me."

Roman didn't want to leave, but Asia's mother propelled him from the room with a firm push.

She could die. The knowledge simmered in the air between them. And that's when Roman knew for sure that Asia meant everything to him. The very idea of trying to live without her was unthinkable. Asia was part of him now. He loved her.

CHAPTER NINE

TWO DAYS LATER

"You will see him," her mother stated. "The orca is decent, even if he is an Anderson." Her brow creased with a hint of confusion. "Some of the Anderson tribe are worthy orcas."

Asia inhaled sharply. Too suddenly, her healing wounds protested. The pain jerked her back to the reality of her situation. "I'm ugly," she rasped. "Scarred." Tears built and overflowed, dripping down both cheeks.

"The orca loves you."

Pain of another sort seared her heart. She swallowed painfully. "He went away."

"I didn't go away willingly," Roman said from the doorway. "My brother shanghaied me. They imprisoned me on the island. I came as soon as I could. How are you?"

Asia stared at Roman, unable to resist looking her fill, filing away memories to pull out when she was alone, when he left her for the final time.

"Fine."

But that was a lie.

She wasn't fine.

The sharks had injured her vocal cords, damaging them badly. It was unlikely she'd ever sing again. The healers had assured her she would speak normally and her speech would become less labored with time. Her body bore several wounds. The healers thought most would heal apart from the ones on her chest. They would scar, and she'd always bear them in memory of the attack.

The bedroom door opened. "Don't go." Too late. The door clicked shut behind her mother, leaving her alone with Roman.

He sauntered closer, moving in the slow strut of his that made her hot. She'd have to get over him. He wouldn't want to marry her, not now with the way she looked. The way she sounded like a croaky duck squawking for breakfast.

Roman perched on the edge of the bed and took her hand in his. His touch seared her flesh, bringing a shiver. His clean, fresh scent of lemons and the outdoors made her weak with longing. She tried to disengage their hands, but he refused to let go.

"What's this nonsense about me not wanting you?" He placed her hand directly on his groin. "Does this feel as though I'm repelled? I love you, babe. I still want to marry you. I'm sorry you can't sing anymore. I know how much you enjoyed it, how good you were at entertaining."

Asia gasped, heat suffusing her cheeks. Was it possible? Her gaze flew to his, and she saw the same longing that festered inside her. She saw acceptance, approval.

Asia saw love.

"Are you sure?" she managed. At least she could talk a little now. The healer kept assuring her the raspy note would lessen with time.

"Positive," Roman said.

Asia struggled upward and slipped from the bed. She'd chosen a loose-necked gown that didn't hug her breasts and irritate her wounds. It also made it easy for the healers to check her injuries. She lifted the hem to display her injuries. "Last chance to run."

"Babe. I'm so sorry." Roman raised his hand and traced the puckered wound that curved around the top of her breast.

Asia bit back a gasp at his touch. Arousal. Heck, he made her want him with a mere touch. "Still want me?" She had to be sure.

"In a heartbeat." He leaned over to brush a kiss on the healing wound at her throat. "Always," he murmured. "I love you, babe. You're not getting away that easily."

The doubt seeped away, replaced by another emotion. Love. "I love you too, Roman."

"About time," he murmured, and he lowered his head and kissed her to seal the bargain. Then, with a grin, he went to the door.

At first, she thought he intended to leave, but he turned the lock and came back to the bed, unfastening the buttons on his shirt as he advanced.

"What are you doing?" Hesitation shaded her voice.

"I need to touch you, so we're going to cuddle. But before we do that, I intend to kiss every one of your wounds."

"You don't want to do that," she croaked.

"Yes, I do." He brushed a lock of hair off her face. "I want to prove how much I desire you."

"I'm ugly."

Roman stripped off the last of his clothes and smiled at her. "Off with the nightgown."

"I...no."

"Please, babe. Do it for me."

Fear hit Asia. The wounds were healing rapidly because of her shapeshifter nature, but they still looked horrid, red and livid. Despite her love for him, the light of approval in his eyes, she worried about her looks. Why did he want her when there were other more beautiful women available, women without scars? Women with musical voices. Before she could dredge up more objections, he urged her to lift her body and whisked off her nightgown. Instinctively, Asia closed her eyes, her muscles tensing in fear.

"Open your eyes, babe." His quiet insistence pushed past her trepidation, and she slowly opened her eyes.

Approval shone in his face, and his mouth curved in a smile. "I love you. I love the person you are inside—your heart. You're generous. Giving. Courageous." He leaned over her and kissed her below one breast, right on top of a red scar. His face showed no distaste, and some of the tenseness dispersed from her body.

She moaned when he traced his fingers along the jagged line. By the time he finished, her body quivered. The lazy stroke of his hands and tongue was driving her crazy.

"Are you too sore to make love?" Once again, he didn't give her the chance to say no. He lifted her so she could straddle his body and gestured at his erection. "Take me inside you. Please."

She couldn't say no. With his touch, he'd made her feel special, and the glow in his eyes did the rest. Any man who could caress and kiss a woman as he'd just done to her was one in love. She truly believed he loved her and it wasn't pity.

Rising up a fraction, she guided his cock to her opening and sank down, impaling herself while he watched her with his keen gaze. She rode him slowly, studying him in return.

"You feel good. Tight. Hot. Perfect." He strummed a finger across her swollen clit while she rocked, driving them both to distraction. She came first with Roman following soon after.

It was perfect, and she'd never felt more loved.

The waves crashed into shore. A gull flew overhead. They walked to the water's edge, paddling as they wandered down the beach.

"Do you think your tribe will ever accept me?" Asia

asked, linking her fingers with his.

"I'll admit it won't be easy at first. Some of the tribe will continue to be suspicious of the Transients. Some of your tribe will feel the same way. Our joint rescue effort and the way your mother assisted with the apprehension of the remaining rebels helped our tribes see we can work together."

"You married me, despite the possible tension and backlash." Asia couldn't keep the troubled note from her voice. "I can't help but worry."

"I love you and couldn't help myself." Roman smiled and squeezed her fingers gently. "Don't worry. Our marriage sends a positive statement. It shows our commitment, our belief in closer relations between our tribes. It tells our people that both tribal leaders accept the idea of change. It's important to show by example."

"But what about Helena's brothers? They're not taking her death well. They're blaming you, accusing you of her murder."

"And most think the shark mercenaries did the deed because she didn't pay them. I have witnesses from both tribes who know I didn't do it because I haven't been alone since your attack. You know that."

Asia nodded, despite her lingering concern for Roman. "Our healers say she was covered with wounds similar to mine."

"And that's what the records will show once the Resident healers do an autopsy on her. Asia, it will work out. We knew our marriage would create tension initially. All we need is time for everyone to get used to the idea."

"I'm happy with you," Asia said. "Very happy."

"Good. I don't want to talk about our tribes. Wanna swim?" Roman drawled.

"I have a better idea." Asia undid the buttons on his shirt, revealing the hard muscles she loved to look at and stroke. She tugged his hand and drew him away from the water. The sand was warm on her bare feet, and the faint breeze stirred her hair.

"And what would that be, Mrs. Anderson?"

They'd sneaked away to marry the previous day, and it still made her giddy thinking about being his wife. "We'll make love, then we'll swim."

Roman shrugged off the shirt, and Asia took a minute to admire the man's broad shoulders and gorgeous tan. This was a big step for her, and judging by the expression on Roman's face, he knew it. So far, apart from the first time when he'd barged into her room, they'd kept their lovemaking in the bedroom with darkness shrouding sight. They hadn't even swum together. Today she wanted to show him she believed in their love.

Asia tugged her T-shirt over her head. She hesitated, allowing the fear to take hold. It grew rapidly, making her want to run. Her scars looked ugly, especially the one around her neck.

"Show me your beautiful breasts."

His gaze was on her cleavage, but then he looked up at her. His dark eyes were full of desire, for her. That gave her courage. Her hands went to the front closure of her bra. She flicked it open and allowed her breasts to spill free. Asia stood, and before her courage waned, she wriggled out of her denim shorts and silky panties.

"You are so lovely, babe. I have to keep reminding myself you're mine." He took her hand and tugged her down to his side. "My woman."

Asia shivered when his hands cupped her breasts. The rough rasp of his fingertips over her flesh made her shiver with anticipation. Between her legs dampened, preparing her for their joining. He rolled a nipple between his fingers. Asia bit back a groan, her desire escalating into a desperate need for more of his touch. So hot. So fast. She needed him.

"Now," she implored. "Don't make me wait."

Roman smiled, a little wickedly. Her pulse rate hiked at the promise inherent in his eyes, his expression. She rolled over on her back and spread her legs without shame. The sun shone down overhead, warming her skin with tiny kisses. She noticed Roman's hands shook as he attempted to remove the last of his clothes. The final doubts dissolved. He really didn't care about her scars and imperfections. All he saw was beauty, someone he loved. *Her*.

"I love you, Roman. I'd like it even more if you made love to me. Now." Her voice was husky, full of emotion, and longing.

Roman chuckled as he joined her on the blanket they'd spread on the sand.

He kissed her and trailed caresses across her jaw, down her neck, scoring the tender skin along her throat and ending with another kiss at one end of a scar. Fire whipped through her as she inhaled the scent of soap and hot male. The stroke of his fingers, followed by his tongue across the curve of one breast, turned her greedy. She wanted it all, and she wanted it now.

Cupping a breast with her hands, she offered it to him, beaming with pleasure when he accepted her impatient prompt. When he sucked a burgeoning nipple into his mouth, she slid her hands down his back, straining upward so he took more of her breast. She luxuriated in the tug of his mouth, the answering pulse between her legs and the juices seeping from her pussy. His touch set her on fire.

She admitted it. The sensations cascaded across her like a shower of warm water.

"Roman," she whispered, shivering when he bit her nipple with a light and exquisite nibble. Pleasure coursed through her body, and she shifted on the blanket, ready to beg him to hurry. "Please, Roman. I need you to fill me, to fuck me now. Please."

"Since you asked so nicely, babe." He paused to kiss her, stroking his tongue into her mouth in a manner that brought to mind sex and thrusts and all sorts of good stuff. "It will be my pleasure. Just as soon as I taste you."

Lifting his head, he grinned at her pout and kissed her way down her body, taking random love bites that made her giggle. Finally, he delved between her legs and used delicate flickers of his tongue to drive her crazy. He licked and sucked, taking her close but not giving her enough to push her over into orgasm.

"Roman?"

"Soon, babe." The wet lash of his tongue punctuated the words, and she quivered, loving the contrast of his soft licks and the rasp of the dark stubble that lined his jaw.

"Payback is a fine thing," she warned.

"So I hear. You can pay me back anytime. Any place." But he lifted his body and buried himself in her hot core with a seamless thrust. Her pussy contracted, clasping him as tightly as her arms wrapped around his neck. Roman was her mate. She was his. They belonged together.

Roman thrust. Once. Twice. Three times. Sensation soared within her, spilling over in incredible pleasure. She shattered with explosive force, felt Roman plunge deep again and come inside her. Oh yeah, they belonged together. They were a team.

Asia sighed in contentment and pressed a lazy kiss against his sweaty shoulder, thinking of the last frantic month.

Two orcas from opposing tribes. Together, they would bring their people together and make the orca shifters a strong race. They'd live on Auckland Island and keep the apartment in the city.

The future—this sea of change—looked bright because together they were one. Currents might run deep, but they ran true, and sleeping with the enemy was the best move she'd ever made.

Like to read some stories from my backlist? Turn the page for a glimpse of *Captured & Seduced*, book one from my House of the Cat series, plus a list of my other releases.

EXCERPT – CAPTURED & SEDUCED

BOOK 1, HOUSE OF THE CAT SERIES

"This plan will work." Yep pulled on his jacket and fastened it securely against the cold. "I feel it in ma bones."

Kaya smirked at her crewmate, her chin-length blue hair swinging against high cheekbones. She tugged Yep's ponytail. "Your bones are sometimes wrong. My research is, however, correct."

Ryman Coppersmith, captain of the *Indefatigable*, ignored them both. He'd already made his decision. He intended to win the hell-horse race on Ornum or at least beat his brother Talor and win their private bet. By the time the race ended, Ry hoped he'd be on the way to clearing his name of murder charges. Talor knew the identity of the murderer, but for some reason had never spoken out, preferring to see Ry exiled instead. Ry scowled. He wanted to go home. He wanted to stride through the streets without fear of capture. He wanted to embrace his sisters and visit his mother's grave.

It was time.

After research on Kaya's part, they'd found the stud farm easily enough. They landed the tender in an empty paddock and emerged to the bite of an icy-cool wind and full darkness.

Ry sniffed the air before striding in the direction of the stud farm. Trees. Grass. Mud. Animals. Every breath he took contained a new scent. The needs of the cat jumped to the fore, and a low rumble eased from him.

"Go ahead," he muttered to his crew. "I will shift."

He knew he sounded curt, but the urgent need to run thrummed through him, even greater than his desire for a woman, and that was bad enough. Blood surged to his cock, the sharp sensation painful and frustrating. No available woman and he refused to fukk any of his crew.

Kaya and Yep melted into the darkness while Mogens, who attracted attention because of his changeable skin color, stayed with the tender. Nanu and Jannike presently orbited Earth in the *Indefatigable*, hopefully remaining undetected.

After a deep inhalation, Ry ripped off his jacket and shirt and let the feline claim him. Trews and boots melted into his body, replaced by black fur. His bones lengthened and shifted, tendons and muscles reforming to the cat. His color vision faded, his surroundings turning to shades of black and white. Ry dropped to all fours and padded across the moist grass, long tail swishing.

As always, a sense of aggravation followed him. Ry knew nothing of his feline background, had never met another of his species. In one pain-filled evening, when he'd thought he might die, he'd turned into a black feline without warning. He'd yowled his panic so loud his shipmates had come running. Ry grinned at the memory. He'd scared them half to death. Although funny now, his unexpected shift into a powerful black cat had been bloody terrifying.

For all of them.

With help from Mogens, the man who'd become their seer and part of the crew, Ry had finally transformed back, bearing a new cat tattoo on his biceps as a souvenir and his shirt in tatters. Weirdly, his trews had survived the transformation. Talk about a learning experience. And he was still learning the foibles of his species. The not knowing scared him. It made him wonder if there had been something else inside the bag they'd found with him as a baby. As a child, he'd asked, but his foster father had told him the bag contained clothes.

The low voices and footsteps of his crew were clearly audible. Ry twitched his nose and prowled after them, annoyed with their casual approach. A sharp feline bark reminded them to reduce the noise. Ry broke into a lope, savoring the play of muscles long confined in humanoid form. The wind ruffled his fur while mud splashed his legs and belly.

When he neared the center of the farm where the owners lived, white post and rail fences carved the land into paddocks. Ry leaped over the nearest, his heart pumping with the physical exertion. An animal snorted, springing into action and galloping from the spot where Ry had frozen in place.

A horse. The Earth counterpart of a hell-horse.

Ry crept along the fence line, not wanting to alarm more animals or attract attention. Once clear, he sped up, muscles moving powerfully, every sense alert. Ry caught the rustle of a small creature in a hedgerow, the tentative neighs of two horses at the far end of a paddock. The chill wind continued to ruffle his fur, the heavy moisture in the air indicating impending rain. Great. Ry hated to get wet. His pace increased to a gallop as he followed the track running between the paddocks.

Ahead, light bled from behind screened windows. According to the information Yep and Kaya had uncovered, the trainer lived with his wife and child. Ry regretted any anguish the trainer's departure would cause and had penned a note, explaining the situation to his family. Hopefully, the Earthlings could decipher the universal language. Ry slipped into the shadows and stalked closer, every sense alert for danger.

A cough over to his left grabbed his attention. Ry stilled, whiskers twitching. The sharp tang of sweat and unwashed body caught the back of his throat. The cough sounded again. A figure staggered from a dim-lit porch and wove to the rails of the nearest paddock. Ry's tension eased. The trainer. He recognized the coat the man wore since it appeared in the photo Yep and Kaya had found during their research on the flight to Earth. A lucky break.

Ry padded closer, placing himself near enough to watch without giving away his presence. He needed to wait for the crew to move into position for the snatch to go smoothly. The man appeared short, about Kaya's height, but solid. His reek said he didn't care much for personal hygiene. His stench didn't bother the horses. Two plodded over to him, and one nuzzled his shoulder. The man smoothed his hand over the glossy neck. The other horse nickered. The man stroked it, and the creatures moved away. Soft footsteps dragged his attention from the man.

Yep indicated the man with a jerk of his head. "He waits for us to extract him and take him on the adventure of his life."

Ry stared, unable to see much despite his superior eyesight. The man wore a cover over his head, obscuring his features from sight. Ry's nose twitched at the objectionable odor coming from the man, the air thick with liquor fumes.

Yep seemed to sense Ry's doubts and sought to reassure. "The man's a champion trainer," he whispered. "Nanu and I attended the races two cycles ago. This man trained five of the twelve winners. Several place getters. Man's natural with the four-legged creatures. Hell-horses should respond to him in the same way."

And if they didn't? Grata, he hated this planet. The cold seeped right to his bones, and the promised rain arrived in a slow drizzle. Ry quaked, attempting to shake off the water without audible noise. Didn't work. Miserable, he shivered, ears flicking while irritation built.

"Aw, frag it," Yep swore. "He's moving."

The man intended to seek shelter. Maybe he wasn't as far-gone as Ry suspected.

Yep slipped after him. Ry followed with a grumbling

sigh, watching the staggering figure with disfavor while he twitched his whiskers. The ground sucked at his paws, the slippery footing making their mission difficult.

The crew moved in, silent signals passing between them until they stood in position. Yep and Kaya converged from opposite sides, springing and disabling the man in well-practiced synchronicity. Kaya pulled the special cloth impregnated with a potion the seer had made from her pocket and pressed it to his nose. The man went limp, and Yep slung the bulky figure over his shoulder before striding in the direction of the tender. Kaya darted up to the shelter and shoved Ry's note under the door before joining Yep.

Ry followed, loping along the muddy track. In a burst of speed, he passed his crew, trying to outrun the returning desire for a woman. It came out of nowhere, unbidden.

Unwanted, the need gripped him with such powerful intensity that he stopped in his tracks. Damn, he'd thought he'd manage for a few more weeks.

Ry tried to ignore the craving writhing through his veins. The out-of-control sensation had intensified during the past few months, affecting his sleep. The constant desire for a woman made his temper uncertain, although he'd managed to hold things together so far. Ry knew his need was escalating to dangerous levels. His attempts to manage what he presumed were feline traits and part of his heritage brought a bark of ironic laughter.

The seer saw his turmoil. The others would realize the tenuous hold he had over his feline if he didn't do something fast. Of course, he'd continue with the search for his people, but in the meantime, he'd have to break down and find a woman to travel with them during their voyage to take the edge off his sexual needs. Hopefully, the woman's presence would slow the downward spiral into the mysterious world of the feline.

The world he didn't understand because he didn't know where he came from or who he was.

Ry raced to the tender and shifted smoothly. His naked chest gleamed with moisture and rivulets of mud, his heart thudded hard and erratic. Inside, Ry ignored his shirt and jacket, preferring to sanitize back on the *Indy* before he redressed.

"Everything okay?" Mogens asked.

"Yeah." Ry wanted to lash out at the seer's scrutiny, tired of the constant analysis. He growled, a vicious snarl of impatience. Ry wanted to laugh at Mogens' undignified scramble to put distance between them but didn't have it in him. "The crew won't be long. Mission accomplished."

The tension inside ratcheted sharply upward. Ry gritted his teeth, wanting to hit someone. Silently, he calculated the length of the flight to the planet Ornum and how quickly he could find a woman. The idea of sinking into the warmth of a female, of licking her fragrant skin and losing himself in the plain rawness of sex, brought an uncontrollable surge of arousal. His cock drew painfully tight, and Ry wheezed through the throbbing ache. He wished he knew what ailed him, why the feline refused to settle even with the suppressant Mogens had made for him.

Footsteps thudded on the tender ramp. Kaya and Yep clattered inside with Yep still carrying the man over his shoulder. He dumped him on the nearest chair and strapped him in for safety. The unconscious human slumped forward, face hidden by the head covering. A noxious smell still emanated from him, the stench compounded in the confined quarters of the tender.

"All aboard." Mogens sealed the entrance. A throaty roar indicated Yep had started up the thrusters, and secs later, they lifted off.

Interested? Learn more at my website.
Captured & Seduced
(https://shelleymunro.com/books/captured-seduced/)

ALSO BY SHELLEY

Middlemarch Shifters

My Scarlet Woman

My Younger Lover

My Peeping Tom

My Assassin

My Estranged Lover

My Feline Protector

My Determined Suitor

My Cat Burglar

My Stray Cat

My Second Chance

My Plan B

My Cat Nap

My Romantic Tangle

My Blue Lady
My Twin Trouble
My Precious Gift
My Grumpy Wolf

Middlemarch Gathering
My Highland Mate
My Highland Fling
My Elusive Mate
My Valiant Princess
My Highland Wedding
My Highland Billionaire

Middlemarch Capture
Snared by Saber
Favored by Felix
Lost with Leo
Spellbound with Sly
Journey with Joe
Star-Crossed with Scarlett

House of the Cat
Captured & Seduced
Claimed & Seduced

Merry & Seduced

Stranded & Seduced

Seized & Seduced

Hunted & Seduced

Festive & Seduced

Betrayed & Seduced

Enticed & Seduced

Dragon Investigators

Blue Moon Dragon

Blood Moon Dragon

Black Moon Dragon

Snow Moon Dragon

Dragon Isles

Liza

Cherry

Rena

Sasha

ABOUT AUTHOR

USA Today bestselling author Shelley Munro lives in Auckland, the City of Sails, with her husband and a cheeky Jack Russell/mystery breed dog.

Typical New Zealanders, Shelley and her husband left home for their big OE soon after they married (translation of New Zealand speak - big overseas experience). A twelve-month-long adventure lengthened to six years of roaming the world. Enduring memories include being almost sat on by a mountain gorilla in Rwanda, lazing on white sandy beaches in India, whale watching in Alaska, searching for leprechauns in Ireland, and dealing with ghosts in an English pub.

While travel is still a big attraction, these days Shelley is most likely found in front of her computer following another love - that of writing stories of contemporary and paranormal romance and adventure. Other interests include watching rugby (strictly for research purposes), cycling, playing croquet and the ukelele, and curling up with an enjoyable book.

Visit Shelley at her website.
https://shelleymunro.com/

Sign Up for Shelley's Newsletter
https://shelleymunro.com/newsletter/